Crits

To my dear friend Mike

from our days with the
National Youth Jazz Orchestra of Great Britain
long, long ago

Penny Lane goes to Italy

David Gordon Rose

RoseTintedSpecs Imprint

RoseTintedSpecs Imprint
Publisher: David G. Rose
Butchers Farm, Molash, Kent, United Kingdom
www.rosetintedspecs.com
email: publisher@rosetintedspecs.com

Printed in the USA. British-English spelling is used in this book.

Introduction

This Penny Lane story is a comedy drama about two Little People (ie., with dwarfism) set in Northern Italy, Switzerland and briefly in Liverpool in the North of England. They are Clementino and Ignatio, twin sons of Count Ferdinand Vespucci. The book begins with an attempt by Clementino one February night to retrieve a promissory note a Zürich bank is witholding by having altered the lock on the family's vault box.

The bank does not want to pay back a seriously large loan the Vespucci family made to them during WWII. Dark forces are behind the refusal. The Vespuccis are unaware a Neo-Nazi organization the secretive *Stalhelm*, still control the bank as they did in the 1940s.

Bank jobs will not go so smoothly if left to amateurs, hence Count Vespucci calling on the services of the discreet and very British Penny Lane Agency. Vespucci was at Oxford University at the same time as Penny Lane. They were fencing partners.

The Agency supplies a new set of keys for the initial attempt, then plans the robbery of the bank over the August holiday in Switzerland. This is not for the money but for Nazi material that will be used to compromise the bank and *Stalhem* if repayment is not forthcoming. The Agency's Italian-speaker Wilson ensures a successful robbery outcome. The brothers hide out in the *palazzo* of their cousin the Countess Anna in St. Moritz-Bad and are nearly captured at the fairground by the Neo-Nazi gang.

There is a strong secondary theme through the story, the love of Clementino and Ignatio for what are considered unsuitable young women, the tall, elegant Sophie and pretty young daughter, Gabrielle of the local shepherd.

Penny Lane, her agency and its team will feature in a series of European adventures, one in each of the member countries of the European Union.

Illustrations

Cover image
Capitano and *Columbina* Masks [thanks to Lady Kelly Hayes]

Penny Lane goes to Italy

This is a tale about the very English (actually, Liverpudlian) Penny Lane Agency helping the venerable Italian Vespucci family pull off a bank robbery in Zürich. It's not the sort of thing this family, any family, does but you will see they have a pressing reason. For the Agency it is another challenge they rise to with legendary attention to detail. This is why they are beloved by the Establishment, in this story, where matters of discretion are paramount.

The events take place over the course of a year not long ago. Since it is also a story of love, passion, jealousy, intrigue and drama in the time-honoured Italian manner I begin with a *dramatis personæ.*

The Principals:

Count Ferdinand Vespucci, a handsome widowed fifty-year old aristocrat. He is head of Pucci Pomodori (tomatoes) and Pucci Pasticceria (cakes and pastry), companies that are household names in Italy, in this story. He lives in a splendid villa near Bergamo in *Lombardia* in North-West Italy with his twin sons and *domestici* (servants) Cook and Lucciano. His servants are a double-act, as are,

Clementino and **Ignatio Vespucci,** the sons. The book is built around these huge characters and their problems with dwarfism, with being Little People. Clementino is older than his twin by twenty minutes and will inherit the title *conte* and estate at Bergamo. There is tension here.

Evasio Vespucci, Ferdinand's younger brother who we don't meet because he is cruising on his doctor's orders. He is responsible for the senior Vespucci company, Pucci Moquette (carpets). It is in financial difficulty and is the main reason why a Vespucci loan to the Swiss bank in the 1940s must be repaid to the family.

Countess Anna, the dark and beautiful cousin who lives with her young son and man-servant in a Seventeenth-century *palazzo* in St. Moritz-Bad in Switzerland. She starts off the story in Zürich, entertains her cousin's sons Clementino and Ignatio at Easter after their twenty-first birthday and shelters them after the August robbery. She also graces the Christmas party at the villa at the end of the story, the *finale* in fact.

Sophie and Gabrielle, the *ragazze* (girls) the boys are hopelessly - and I choose the word carefully - in love with. You won't forget these young women either.

Then there are:
Saltzmann the Zürich banker. He is how you expect a banker to be.

Baron Rothenfelder, dyed-in-the-wool Nazi and boss of the thuggish Neo-Nazi *Stalhelm* that controls the bank. The story is driven by Rothenfelder and the organization bent on bullying its way out of repaying the war-time loan made to the bank by Vespucci's father. They think because the family is Italian it will not get its act together over the matter. Robbing banks is beyond even Vespucci eccentricity, hence,

Penny Lane, the Liverpool Lady, CEO of Penny Lane Agency whom Vespucci calls upon for technical support. He is acquainted with Miss Lane from their days at Oxford University when they fenced and occasionally took tea together. We assume she is eventually paid for her services in what is ostensibly Vespucci ingenuity.

Wilson, Miss Lane's Italian-speaking assistant. He is worthy of a mention, since almost everything relating to this job, the robbery and escape with the spoils is effected by him.

Here then, is my tale **Penny Lane goes to Italy** beginning one recent February and ending on Christmas night the same year.

Snow fell for most of the drive from St. Moritz to Zürich that February morning. The journey was tedious but it provided the perfect excuse for missing the flight to New York. Anna played with her fur as she went over the plan of this ridiculous robbery once again. She was not a liar. An actor certainly but not a liar. She looked at her watch, instructed Emil to turn toward the city centre and inspected her face. She would normally have consulted her chauffeur on how she looked, he was after all her best critic but he had been bitchy all morning and she was not in an indulging mood.

Emil negotiated the Corniche through the heavy traffic along Bahnhofstraße into the town's old quarter at the top of the lake. It was one o'clock as they drew up outside the grey anonymous frontage of one of the city's two hundred banks. Emil set about buffing his nails, a thin smile gracing his lips. Though the *contessa* was not suited to her good name at risk once again, he had no reservations. When she made up her mind no-one stood a chance.

Wishing her luck, he chose then to suggest she had applied too much foundation.

"A heavy make-up called 'Luck' would have its uses ..." Anna responded sweetly. She could not think of any woman who could not use it regularly. "Yes, I like it. Put it in the Business Ideas book will you, Darling ..."

The *Contessa* Anna Raffino di Bergamo, Italian by birth now living in Switzerland, widowed and immensely wealthy stepped into the swirling snow of a winter afternoon before the marble portal of the Saltzmann Schweinchencommerzbank. She smiled in a predatory manner at the young employee who appeared with a large umbrella, drew the collar of her fur coat up to emphasise her eyes and made her entrance.

The bank's owner and director-general Christian Saltzmann, a corpulent middle-aged man with a small moustache, stumbled on the stairs when he saw the countess. He greeted her with a salacious smile and indicated to his staff he would take charge. Though used to men fawning in her company, Anna considered this one weaker than most and even a practised smile was difficult to maintain.

She went through her story about missing the early flight to New York without elaboration. As she had explained earlier over the telephone she would prefer somewhere safer than a hotel for the overnight storage of valuable artefacts. The aluminium flight trunk she had brought with her from St. Moritz-Bad was transferred from the Rolls-Royce to the main vault with due ceremony. Its safe keeping, Saltzmann insisted, being the least the bank could do for the countess.

As they were about to leave the white marble vault that was empty except for her trunk of a metre in height and a little over a metre in length, like a sarcophagus flanked by orderly rows of chromium steel boxes, Saltzmann dabbed his forehead with a handkerchief the size of a dish cloth. The sickly smile reappeared and Anna knew he was unable to contain his vulgar curiosity. She could see him recounting her story of the bad weather, of missing the flight to New York and having to re-book the trunk for the following day.

"Please forgive my enquiring into your affairs *contessa* but are these not the items of pottery from your Chinese collection due in next month's sale?"

Anna smiled tightly.

"Not pottery, *Herr* Saltzmann, porcelain, Ming porcelain. A pair of *Ch'eng Hua* vases that were a gift to my family from the Empress Dowager herself."

Saltzmann watched her unfasten the top three clasps of her mink, pull a key on a gold chain slowly from her cleavage and muttered weakly,

"They must be very beautiful ..."

It was a full hour before Anna was able to relax in a comfortable chair by a wood-burning stove in the nearby Widder Hotel. A coffee and pastry was placed before her. She had no intention of eating the pastry and the coffee was not good for her composure but she was comfortable with these trappings and elegant surroundings.

The trunk containing the Ming vases, actually one Ming vase, was now lodged in the bank's main vault. Her visit to the premises a month earlier was when the robbery had actually commenced. Her task on that occasion had been to access her box and secure an impression of the bank's master key.

A senior clerk had the responsibility of placing this key in the door alongside the client's key. He would then wait discretely at the vault's circular entrance. It was almost miraculous the countess, with the tiniest piece of dentist's moulding wax around the back of one of her rings, got a part-impression of the master key while the clerk was still holding it.

It had not been enough for her cousin Ferdinand to secure a copy. It was, however, good enough for the Penny Lane people to complete the job, along with providing six new client keys, each slightly different. This was the stage they had reached that afternoon.

The reason for needing new keys was because her cousin had been unable to access his private box at the bank for months. One day in November, his key suddenly, ridiculously, did not fit. The lock had been tampered with. Disagreement with the bank over the cause of this had reached the stage of legal proceedings.

There was some urgency in Ferdinand's need to access his papers. Among them was a promissory note showing the bank owed his side of the Vespucci family, he and his brother Evasio, a substantial amount of money. That request matured in August, after which another year would have to pass before any withdrawal of funds and accrued interest could be made. This was if the bank was amenable and if the senior Vespucci business survived.

The original investment in Saltzmann's bank in 1942 by Ferdinand and Evasio's father, Anna's uncle, had grown over 60 years to 800 million Swiss Francs. It was a sum not to be sneezed at. There was now a touch of desperation within the family on the need for its return.

Ferdinand had been absolutely correct in insisting she did not deviate from the story, Anna recalled. The vulgar little banker knew immediately it was those wretched vases on their way for auction.

Ferdinand had also guessed that Saltzmann, who had a collection of *chinoiserie* of his own, would be unable to resist asking if he could see them and that it would be perfect if he did. Looking in to the upper part of the trunk, that is.

Dear Ferdinand. There was no doubt there were things one needed a man like him for.

She was about to ask the *Hotelrezeptionistin* to bring her a telephone when she remembered the call to Bergamo on the outcome that afternoon should be made from a public box. She picked up the receiver in a booth in the foyer but could not be bothered with the instructions on making international calls. When she realised it also needed money, a card, she lost interest completely. Emil would have to do it.

1/2

Count Ferdinand Vespucci had been pacing around the library of his villa in the mountains north of Bergamo since lunchtime that day. Everything had gone like clockwork from his end but he had not had to spin a cock-and-bull story to the manager of a Swiss bank for some time. He did however feel that sympathetic support over this 'robbery' was as vital as any other.

When the message came from Zürich that everything had gone smoothly he rang down to the kitchen for his tomato juice aperitif. Lucciano, a fixture in the Vespucci household before Ferdinand was born, appeared with a silver tray. Before giving the aperitif its final dash of something from a little green bottle, he waited for the count to straighten his bow-tie and brush a fine moustache with the miniature Mason-Pearson he had bought in Harrods many years before.

Vespucci was a handsome, distinguished aristocrat with greying temples and archetypal Italian good looks. He was a keen sportsman and climber, like his two sons and therefore different from most middle-aged Italians in being superbly fit. He was well-liked for his generosity, his geniality and dry wit. An ailing family fortune and imminent midnight assault on a Swiss bank by his eldest born had rendered him uncharacteristically quiet.

When Lucciano returned to his duties Vespucci looked across his estate, savouring the aperitif. He had never asked about the addition that gave the drink its kick, knowing he wouldn't be told anything other than it was an "old Neapolitan pick-me-up." The sun was weaker across the terrace and snow-covered vineyards with the mountains almost in silhouette. How fortunate they were to have an estate in a regional park, the *Parco delle Orobie Bergamasche*.

It did not ameliorate his anxiety that afternoon. A mixture of admiration and guilt over what he was putting his eldest son through for family honour remained uppermost in his mind. He telephoned the kitchen once more with instructions on the wine he wanted served at dinner, something a little more special he said. The least he and his second born, Ignatio, could do was drink to Clementino's success that night. The lad could not have been remotely comfortable in the trunk.

Late that evening deep underground in the very heart of Zürich, Clementino looked cross-eyed at the watch he had bought for the occasion, one with an LED display he could read easily in total darkness. It showed 22:34. He had been on his back for more than ten hours unable to turn more than a few centimetres. He was not supposed to leave the trunk until after midnight but he could bear it no longer. He undid the latches securing the lower side panel and hinged it open.

Breathing a sigh of relief even though the vault was surprisingly stuffy, he listened carefully before beginning a much-practised shuffle to get himself out of the trunk. Sitting on the floor eventually in the darkness with a bright red 22:34 still showing wherever he looked he started on his massage routine. He was so stiff he could hardly move and didn't know what he would do if someone chose then to enter the vault.

When he was feeling more comfortable he reached into his bag for the torch. There were other essentials in it, a comb, bread, *prosciutto* and a drink Cook had packed but he left these untouched.

He didn't want to unwrap his lunch in case people wondered why Ming vases should smell of ham.

When he switched on the torch he almost wished he hadn't. The light glinted on the handles and escutcheons on the rows of boxes of chrome and polished steel. The vault was bigger than he had imagined and though this was Switzerland and the inside of it clean like an operating theatre, it was disconcertingly like a morgue. Creeping up on him was the memory of his brother locking him in the cellars at the villa with the rats. It was one of the best worst-twenty-minutes-of-their-life scenarios they both strove to improve on. That one hadn't bothered Clementino of course, though he did call his brother "Ratfink" for some time afterwards, a word he had gleaned from their collection of British Victorian Penny Dreadfuls.

He checked his watch again. It was approaching eleven and the changeover of security shifts and he had to stick to the plan. There was no camera in the vault and it was time-locked until eight in the morning but they knew Saltzmann worked long hours, even over the weekend, occasionally until his witching hour of midnight. Clementino could not start fiddling with new keys until after midnight. Reluctantly he wriggled back into the trunk.

Eleven passed. There was no sound. Twenty more minutes went by and it occurred to him that if the walls of the vault were a couple of metres thick then of course he would hear nothing. A rat scratching, maybe. He played with the idea of the noise numbers of rats might make and peering at his watch again was relieved to see it was past midnight. He eased himself once more out of the lower compartment and began preparations for the task of the night. A job he noted with satisfaction that could only be done by someone of diminutive proportions.

Above Clementino there were things happening that none of them involved in this escapade could even have dreamed of. At eleven, a light glowed on the console in the security office. The afternoon man whose shift was just ending asked for identification from the uniformed officer whose face was distorted by the street camera's wide-angle lens. It was Herman, of course and he would normally have exchanged some banter with his mate before going down to let him in. After an evening meeting, the Old Man said he would be in until late. He was standing beside him in the security office, his usual sober self.

It certainly would not suit Herman who enjoyed the simple pleasure of the night shift of sitting almost literally on one of the biggest wads in town. A bit of a lad, a *ziemlicher kerl*, he knew how girls could be charmed by talk of high finance, bank notes stacked to the ceiling and 'more gold than in Fort Knox,' even if he could only pull a few francs from his pocket. It worked for him and the occasional bright-eyed lass was let in for a little tour and reciprocal peek at her goodies.

It was approaching midnight when Saltzmann on the floor above Security cleared the last of his work concerned with the city's Institute of Bankers. One task remained, necessitating a trip down to the vault. Smoothing his hair, he shifted the antique gas fire a fraction with his foot and moved a small lever inside the fireplace. A panel in the wall adjacent to the chimney breast clicked open and he squeezed his rotund figure into the cavity behind it. Before him was an iron rung ladder.

It was an old building and the hiding space was constructed in the late Sixteenth Century after decades of warring between Protestant Zürich and neighbouring Catholic Cantons. Under Saltzmann family ownership the hiding place was extended at the beginning of Switzerland's Civil War in 1847 to a now long-gone ground floor fireplace. It was extended again in the 1930s to the city's sewer system. Now it was sealed just above this at the bank's main vault on the lower ground floor.

Saltzmann grunted as he began the four-floor descent to attend to a matter that had come to the end of the initial stalling process. The Vespucci solicitors had used the word *grottesco* about the family key 'suddenly' not fitting the door to the family's vault box and had applied for a court order for its opening. Since it concerned the repayment of a vast sum of money from *Stalhelm* funds the order for the second stage, the removal of the promissory note from the box, had been given. The coded instruction had come that evening directly from Würzburg.

Clementino, meanwhile was humming a little tune. Reluctant to bring out the big flashlight in case it had to be stuffed back into the trunk he decided he could manage by the light of his key ring torch. He was having trouble. The master key delivered to Papa one morning by an Englishman in an almost laughably inappropriate hunter's hat with large *piuma*, turned easily in the vault box. Of the other six keys the one that showed promise was still very stiff. Each had been cut differently after the canny family solicitor had ascertained with a smear of hair cream on the family's original key one tooth had been altered.

Clementino didn't want to force it. On the other hand he really wanted to open the box. Sweat trickled down his brow but with perseverance he got it to turn the two revolutions. He pulled open the door in a moment of triumph, then shut it again. Something inside had moved.

He went stone cold as a faint noise turned into a vigorous scraping before there was silence once again. It was yet another worst-twenty-minutes, on par with having slipped in a steep gulley with a bush saving his life but having to drop his gear bit by bit as the bush eased out of the crevice.

At first he reasoned the box had been booby-trapped. It might have been a rat smelling his packed lunch. Marginally worse was a bank devil up to its tricks. Most likely some swine had just rifled their safety deposit box from the other side. Could it now be the filching of the promissory note? If he had not been in a Swiss bank vault with a set of keys in the dead of night he would have thought the accessing of deposit boxes from their rear just too far-fetched for words.

He edged open the door and peered from the blackness into an even blacker hole. Cool air bathed his clammy face and yet another realization of how amateurish they were occurred to him, the probability the vault had no ventilation and he might have suffocated.

Masking his torch with his fingers he pointed it into the box. The back was open slightly and the black tin deed box had indeed been withdrawn. He lifted out what remained, documents, bonds, jewellery and placed it in neat piles on the floor. He needed to investigate further.

The compartment looked big enough to accommodate him but proved a very tight fit. Standing on the trunk which he had dragged across the floor, he let out his breath and pulled himself in. The rear flap was heavy but using his new wriggling technique, testing all the while he could reverse himself, he got his head through the back end.

His light showed a wall of rough brickwork and a narrow passage the length of the vault. On the back of the vault wall were large rusty levers that coincided no doubt with the deposit boxes. How absolutely frightful and how ingenious he thought. Most interesting was the bottom of an iron ladder at the end of the corridor. Further, he decided, he would not venture.

His withdrawal in fits and starts almost proved his undoing. He lost a shoe. The front of his sweat-shirt rode up and almost strangled him but at last inside the vault he replaced the papers and things in exactly the same order, locked the box door, slid the trunk back to the pencil marks he had made on the floor and waited.

It was two o'clock and he was wondering if he had missed the noises from within the box when they started up, accompanied once more by shafts of light escaping through the keyholes that made him duck. When he opened the compartment this time, there was the deed box with the Vespucci family crest of boar, cherries and bejewelled coronet with nine pearls, emblazoned in silver, red and gold. His heart was thumping. Were his worst fears about the note about to be realised?

He was certainly not asleep when his wristwatch alarm shattered the silence at 07:30. He was sitting astride the trunk in the darkness rocking back and forth gritting his teeth. The alarm was a good bit of planning, as people would also have wondered why Ming vases should be snoring. More appropriate would have been the including of a wee bag in his kit and not a little one. With at least an hour before he could escape into the boot of the car he was in desperate need of a toilet.

He had been confined for twenty hours and although he had only sipped a little mineral water he was on the point of bursting. He had been crossing his legs and jumping up and down for a couple of hours. He alternated hot and cold. He was in fact, in a terrible state and now with less than half an hour before the vault door opened he knew he had no choice. He opened the upper part of the trunk with his spare key, dragged out several handfuls of the polystyrene granules packing the vase and in a moment he could only describe as ecstatic, relieved himself.

He was just too embarrassed to look at what he was doing to a rare piece of porcelain of a delicate under-glaze blue with jewel-like touches of red, green and yellow about the designs.

'... they must be very beautiful ...' he recalled Saltzmann saying. 'Not beautiful, *Herr* Saltzmann. They are exquisite,' Anna replied, 'a truly perfect statement of fine porcelain ...'

With only six minutes to opening time Clementino suffered a more ordinary heart-stopping moment. He could not shut the trunk lid. He stuffed polystyrene granules down his tracksuit bottom. Still the lid would not close. A loud buzzer startled him. He had one more go, knowing he would have only seconds to try and break the vase with the big torch. The latches clicked shut. He had just about squeezed into the lower section when dazzling neon lights showed beads on the floor. He reached out as the huge circular vault door edged open, grabbed them and sealed himself in. All he could hear after this was his heart pounding. Mercifully, nothing else happened.

He didn't think he would be quite so glad to hear Anna half an hour later. There was a shuffling of feet and he felt himself levitated. It would be a few minutes more before he could escape into the boot of the Rolls-Royce, unless there was a hitch and he really did not want to travel cargo to New York.

Penny Lane goes to Italy

2/1

A damp, earthy smell mixed with the agreeable aroma of wood smoke hung in a delicate balance around the Vespucci villa. Beyond the gardens and outbuildings lay extensive vineyards and orchards that were still harbouring patches of snow. Far down the valley was the old town of Bergamo and beyond that a miserable, fogbound Milan.

Clementino, on the corner of the West terrace and wrapped well against the cold of early March, dabbed his brush absently into the glass of Grappa and hot water Lucciano had brought him. He was having trouble with his watercolour 'Sunrise in the Valte' now it was nearer sunset. He was tired too, having risen early for the event. Only the strangled cries of his brother practising up the south face of the villa with some new climbing equipment was disturbing the magnificence of the mountain scenery.

It had been three weeks since his futile attempt at recovering the promissory note with, by any reckoning, the bank winning the battle to hang on to it. Three weeks of torment at the villa with little digs from his brother, his father silent and troubled and months wasted on planning what should have been an ingenious recovery. It had been close but his sense of duty and the fact there was now no proof of a vast amount of money owed to the family only added up to failure.

"Tino, I say … Tino …"

Irritated by his brother's bleating, Clementino put his paint box down, flung the end of a ridiculously long scarf over his shoulder and strode around the expansive marble terraces of the Seventeenth-century villa. His eyes scanned the portico on the south side and pool of rope before the studded bronze doors. Above the elaborate cornice was a line of carved statuettes. Above these, dangling upside down in the wintry sunshine and framed by a massive stone pediment showing the hunting of wild boar, was Ignatio. Rope trailed like spaghetti from the roof. Typically, his brother's foot was caught in it.

"So why don't you grab Bacchus's grapes?"

"I did ... they broke off ..." came the plaintive reply. "His head's loose as well."

"Try a rope around your neck."

"Cad ..."

"Then you'll just have to cut something off before it freezes." Ignatio watched his brother disappear around the western end of the villa and even insults failed him. He had come to the end of making allowances for Clementino's hostility just because their Trojan Horse ploy hadn't worked.

As the sun slipped upside down beyond the snow-capped peaks toward Switzerland taking the temperature with it, he pondered Elder's cryptic words. Even if he was a smart-arse who pansied around painting most of the time, he was a good climber.

Now at sunset the answer to his predicament dawned on him. He located the oversize Swiss Army knife in his new mountaineering jacket with its duck-down lining and cut the laces of the boot caught in the ropes. The boot shot upwards as though on elastic, he lurched right side up and grimaced as the knife bounced off the cornice, clattering on the shadowy terrace far below from where Lucciano was tutting vigorously about a baroque facade by Longhena being used for climbing practice. Ignatio heard the old servant but was unable to reply. He was now caught in four intertwining lines and had begun to spin.

All was peaceful that dusk, save for the squawking of magpies and Ignatio's continuing problems expressed in the politest terms. Only Clementino heard the distant humming of a tourer winding its way up the valley road, its gears changing frequently and deftly. Along the section long known as the flying kilometre the tomato-red Ferrari, the 'flying tomato' appeared, lights blazing. It went into a ten-metre slide, peppering henhouse and tractor shed with gravel and came to rest in the correct position for a similarly vigorous getaway. Cars should be driven, Papa said often and demonstrated frequently.

Clementino put his paints down and rinsed his brush, wondering where the Grappa had gone. His father did not see him in the half light and passed through the portico taking a black cloud with him to the house.

Clementino and Ignatio were aware of the situation with the senior Pucci company, Pucci Moquette. Papa had been at the Milan factory all day with lawyers working on separating some of the complicated finances by which the Pucci companies were interlinked. Uncle Evasio was the chief executive of the carpet and textiles. They knew if the carpets were pulled from under them the rest of the Pucci business would be in trouble.

Clementino had no time to dwell on the matter. The whine of nylon passing through a figure of eight descender caused him to roll backwards reflexively. A boot missed him by a hair's breadth. Easel and 'Sunrise' went flying and Ignatio landed with all the characteristics of a demon except the smoke.

"So, Elder, you would see me hang upside down through dinner ..."

The menace in Ignatio's voice was negated by his wearing only one boot and Clementino could not resist the comment,

"… time to buy the train ticket for the North Face of the Eiger …"

Ignatio, eyes blazing freed himself from his carabiners and lashed out with his foot and dangling sock. Clementino laughed theatrically then countered with a blow to the chest. Ignatio fell backwards against the base of a fountain, struggled to his feet, leapt awkwardly into the fountain and discovered water in it. Clementino, imprudently vaulted in after him.

Now really wet and cold Ignatio still managed to snigger at his brother wearing a Homburg, the stupid scarf and Grandfather's greatcoat clinging to him down to his ankles and told him he looked more like Toulouse Lautrec every day. Incensed, Clementino tried a kick, steadying himself by grabbing an appendage on the bronze athlete in the centre of the fountain. He was mortified when it broke off but managed to tip his upstart brother back onto the flagstones. Ignatio remained where he was, already planning his revenge. Lucciano was shuffling rapidly in their direction.

Vespucci stood impassively at the library window watching his sons shake hands grudgingly. It had been a long time since tension between them had come to blows. He would be having words with them. He picked up a photograph of their mother, his beloved Margherita. She would not have tolerated her boys behaving like street urchins. Neither would she have tolerated the root cause, the 800 million Swiss francs, 650 million Euros, owed by the Saltzmann bank. They were stalling and she would have had plenty to say about it.

The problem became pressing over the winter with the ailing health of his younger brother. He headed a senior business massively in debt, along with many others due to the demise of textile manufacturing around Europe. Although Ferdinand's responsibilities, Pucci Pomodori and its range of tomato products and Pucci Pasticceria and its cakes, biscuits and pastries were flourishing, it was confirmed that afternoon his liquidity and his ability to raise capital was not sufficient to save the senior company.

He turned to the window with his afternoon Bloody Mary and

his pathos turned to displeasure. The bronze figure gracing the fountain was spouting water over the flagstones with Lucciano fussing around it. The boys were in need of a reminder of the privileges of owning Roman antiquity as well as the futility of scrapping. It had been a long while since he had referred to them as Romulus and Remus, his feral children. Soon it would be time for them to be off and found their own cities. Chroma, perhaps. Even Ignezia.

That they were currently not friends was clear with their distinct lack of interest in the *Carnevale di Bergamo* at the end of February where parties and get-togethers with their friends would lift them all out of winter. It was confirmed by nothing at all happening at the villa on *Primo d'Aprile* a couple of weeks laters, when he and the staff would normally be locking their doors and looking over their shoulder. Only Cook marked the occasion with a *ravioli al pesce d'aprile*, 'April Fool Ravioli' for lunch.

2/2

Five weeks after the robbery attempt, into April now and just before Easter, preparations for the occasion of the twenty-first birthday of Clementino and Ignatio were finalised. After their coming-of-age party at the villa they would be driving to Switzerland for the last skiing and first walking, staying with their relative the *Contessa* Anna at her *palazzo* in St. Moritz-Bad. It was Anna's treat as she was unable to attend their party.

The birthday which fell that year on Good Friday was a big event in the calendar of *Lombardia* High Society. It was a good time for such a celebration and Vespucci put money problems aside. The vines were wired up and fruit trees down the valley were covered in blossom. The birthday also saw the maturing of various financial trusts and Vespucci thought ten o'clock in the morning as good a time as any for the required father-to-sons talk.

The two boys stood before their papa in the study. Ignatio, just visible behind the huge desk, cut a dashing figure in his tweed jacket with its neat little elbow pads. He was sporting a pale blue silk cravat and matching breast pocket handkerchief. He was also wearing his British-made moleskin breeches that buttoned at the knee, smart Jaeger socks and the custom-made Zamberlan mountain boots he invariably wore because his papa suspected, they gave him more height.

Clementino Vespucci, the more sophisticated, more intelligent of the twin boys and heir by twenty minutes to the title *conte* and family estate climbed on to a chair. He was puffing an oval Turkish cigarette through his grandfather's ivory and gold-banded holder, his wavy hair swept back emphasising his suave looks. Such mature young sons Vespucci thought, big in heart, if small in stature. Mama would have been so proud of them, even if they were Little People.

When he had offered his congratulations and handed over the documents transferring the responsibility of their trusts, he shook their little hands and bent to embrace them. Both thanked their father but did not need to look at the figures. Papa had been above board in all things relating to family finances since they could remember.

They were also directors of the *pasticceria* and *pomodori* brand names. They didn't work at company headquarters in Milan but attended meetings frequently and had taken their responsibilities seriously from an early age. Ignatio was Technical Director and Clementino Artistic Director. They knew their jobs well, having been promoted to these positions when four years old.

By the age of five they had learnt that lots of pocket money bought lots of things. By six they realised that effort enabled them to buy things their friends could only dream of. By eight, fed up with *dolciumi* and *giochi intelligente*, 'sweets' and 'smart toys,' they had settled into a routine of homework from school and selected 'problems' relating to the company. They also began building a rocket that would take them to the Moon.

They were fortunate in being able to work from home. Clementino had his art and design studio next to his attic bedroom on the north-west side of the villa. Ignatio, also in the attic and facing south-east had a well-equipped laboratory, kitchen and roof garden adjacent to his.

Vespucci looked at his boys in a moment of silence, hoping there was not some mad scheme, such as the rocket, they might have for spending their inheritance on. Then he relaxed. What did it matter, what indeed could he do? They were sensible boys and they seemed to be thinking ahead regarding direction and goals. With the exception of girlfriends.

He could have done with his wife's wisdom on this matter. How insistent would she have been in their boys marrying young women of *una famiglia nobile* or of *elevato ceto sociale*, of suitable families, even? Perhaps she would have said these things were no longer relevant and both should choose partners they loved. He found such things difficult to work through and did appreciate the occasional advice from his cousin in St. Moritz-Bad.

While this little man-to-man was in progress, Lucciano was struggling up the staircase with Champagne, glasses, lobster mousse *tartine* and caviar. The study was not the place for *antipasti* and drinks, twenty-first birthday or not. When he had served one bottle and joined in an informal toast he was dispatched to fetch a second. Cook came up with the third and last bottle of Krug Grande Cuvée in the cellar to see what was going on and found all the men in tears at the suggestion by the boys they would gladly give over their inheritance if it would solve the company's financial problems. Vespucci had calculated it would not but did not say this. This was how Good Friday began.

The buffet was an immediate hit as the celebrations got under way that evening. Cook and probably her entire living family had moved around the kitchen like a whirlwind for days with both the party and Easter Sunday coming up. The wine flowed and the band took it away with a Glen Miller selection beginning with an appropriate A String of Pearls, considering the number of elegant *giovane donna* wearing them that evening.

Ignatio was still suffering from a lunchtime hangover struggling with the smell of alcohol, a mountain of food and two hundred larger-than-life, over-the-top of his head people, whether friends and their friends or not. When the orchestra began playing and he should have been circulating in the ballroom, he was to be found on the terrace looking across the mountains to where his heart really lay, with his Gabrielle, his *Ninfa della Montagna del Nord.*

Actually, she was from the last village up the valley before the high mountains but he liked to be poetic about it, about his misery at being apart from his *ragazza* and at their joy on meeting. It had been a month exactly since they had last snatched time together. It was getting worse. They were really beginning to miss each other when apart. They were actually feeling pain.

He managed a smile in the darkness and cool of the evening when a school friend, Francesca, appeared and congratulated him on his now adult status.

"But don't go all grown-up on us suddenly like your brother did on our first day at school!"

She was wearing a lovely old-fashioned pink chiffon party dress with petticoats, pink shoes and unfortunately, a large pink bow in her hair. Grabbing his arm she pressed herself close, asking how she might cheer him up. Just her laughing and giggling as they talked was enough, Ignatio said and he was grateful.

She was curious about their risqué party invitations ending in English *"... bring a friend, if you have one!"*

"The replies made good reading," Ignatio said smiling, "especially when we have been in the dumps here lately. Perhaps you would help me present the prize for the wittiest response? It's between *we'll come to your 21st, as you won't be having another ... I'll bring two, as you'll probably need one* and *... do any of us have friends? Maybe it'll be just you and me, Kid(s) ..."*

Francesca implored him to join in the fun and not let the party fade. And about Clementino she said with some concern, "he's already sitting on Sophie's lap by a punch bowl big enough for him to swim in."

Ignatio left short-sighted Fran peering at a watch too crowded with diamonds to see the time by and wandered over to the buffet.

There he was, the adult Clementino, always more discreet, more reserved and a touch more cautious. He had limited his drinking to the celebratory toast in the study. During a late lunch in the kitchen with Lucciano and Cook he was the one who reminded Papa they were only Little People. Much as they might like to think Champagne flowed through their veins he quipped, a bottle each and it would do just that.

He was therefore able to greet the first of their guests that evening with a giant balloon glass of one of his cocktails, vintage Champagne, a *virgini* Marsala, *crème de menthe* and light and dark cherries from the estate. The point of the glass was to swish it around frequently and enjoy the 'legs' and bobbing fruit. Ironically he called this cocktail 'Legless.' A head and the need to lie down came later, after a lot of it, he would say. For its actual drinking he used a striped straw provided by the maid, a special one, she said. She knew he wouldn't know it came from MacDonald's.

The mood of the two brothers had undergone a subtle reversal. Ignatio got a grip on himself after being rescued by Francesca while Clementino let himself go, just a little. At around ten o'clock he was indeed in the ballroom with the ladies by a table carrying enough alcoholic liquor to be of concern to the local *vigile del fuoco*. His friend Sophie, to whom he had been escort all evening had taken charge.

The ladies were once again terribly amused at him sitting on her lap spouting tall stories. He had related his exploits as a missionary among Pigmy tribesmen in the Congo. There was the time he was asked to be a *Babbo Natale* more readily identifiable to small children at Christmas. He may even be related to Pepin the Short, King of the Franks, he said matter-of-factly who, in 754 took back a great part of Lombardy, returning it to the ousted Pope Stephen II. It didn't always go down well that this gesture laid the foundation of the Papal State and enduring power of the Catholic Church. He could hardly not throw in mention of Pepin's illustrious father, Charles Martel and son, Charlemagne who was crowned the first Holy Roman Emperor on Christmas Day 800.

The title *conte*, he also never tired of telling, emanated from the

Latin word for 'military companion.' Vespucci comital territory in feudal times included a huge tract of Lombardy extending into Switzerland. He was still researching how small the early Mongolian Appaloosas were at the time and just how big could Genghis Khan have been to sit on one for weeks on end. He would hardly have been a buffalo on a bean, as their grandmother used to say. He must have been a little bloke.

Clementino had known Sophie since they were sixteen years old and she was having her coming-out party. She was also celebrating coming top in every subject in her final year at school. Clementino had the identical accolade he had celebrated the week before.

The attraction was not this particular *signorino* and *signorigna* being too clever by half. Neither was it the fact she was a natural blonde with blue eyes, which was unusual in an Italian girl from the South. The moment that would be with him forever was when Sophie came up to him at her party and said she thought every handsome man had asked her to dance.

They had been partners many times in the five years since but it was a huge emotional burden knowing he would never be able to ask Sophie for her hand in marriage. She was invariably in the company of some sophisticated *debuttante* or partying the night away with society's other bright young females. It was a simple agony Clementino endured. Sophie's coming out also signalled her preference for girls.

Later still, when it was no longer amusing he should be sitting on the lap of a statuesque blonde, for she was almost two metres in height and would have been Italy's tallest model had her father permitted such a career path, Sophie led her diminutive friend onto the dance floor. He wasn't allowed to touch her, which would have been trying to get his arms around her hips. It was cupped hands only and formal dancing but she always smelt divine from where he was, halfway down her body and he would soon be a balloon again floating off into the night on waves of sexual fantasy, until his hangover sank him.

When it was almost eleven o'clock and the party was livening up,

Ignatio detached himself from a group of friends and escaped onto the north loggia to avoid Francesca, though he didn't mean to be rude. Like her namesake *Santa Francesca Romana*, the patron saint of motorists, she was very kind and a popular passenger on car journeys even though she couldn't read signs or see cars on the wrong side of the road.

He passed his brother in the ornamental gardens among couples canoodling under lanterns and overheard him at an unusual stage of indiscretion. He was pleading with Sophie and a bevy of beautiful girls to pose for him in the nude, for the sake of art, all of them together as Sabines if they wanted some attention, or Caryatids if they fancied something to do.

He also overheard his friend Luigi in animated discussion with his English girlfriend, denying Italians have a fixation about coffee.

"... it 'as to be *cappuccino* at breakfast. Before work a *macchiato*. If I 'ave clients I 'ave something stronger, a *stretto*. I 'ave to walk two blocks for a good one. And when I was in England, you English 'ad never 'eard of a *granita di caffè con panna! Per favore ...*"

Grimly Ignatio pulled a cloak around his shoulders and hurried up the hill in the chilly night air to the orchards and vineyards. From the top he could just make out the second most beautiful house on

the estate, a miniature Nineteenth-century château in the French style.

Its shutters needed repairing and its roof renewing. Nevertheless, he loved the house and its commanding view over the valley that was better even than the villa's. No-one had lived in it since the estate manager in 1927, himself an aristocrat, though the grounds were kept tidy and it was opened every Spring for essential maintenance. This house would be their home when they were married, he told Gabrielle.

She knew the house, of course and said it was big and beautiful but the idea was beyond her comprehension. To keep her interested he told her occasionally he had put yet more pocket money towards it. He didn't tell her it would actually be paid for with a last instalment from his inheritance. Neither did he mention his next big concern, the cost of its renovation.

"No *villino* for my *ragazza*," he said decisively. "We will live in a *castello*."

She had warmed to them keeping a menagerie of miniature animals on the hills around the house. She requested a herd of Falabella horses that would roam the backyard and Breton *Ouessant* sheep and rams, the smallest in the world, to dot the hillsides. They would surely be able to find room for some English Babydoll lambs. Miniature Schnauzers could guard the compound.

He fancied a gang of delinquent miniature Mexican Hairless, African Pygmy and Juliani pigs he would have to stride out to with gaucho trousers and wide-brimmed hat, whip in hand to bring to order. The last pig he had been left in charge of was a huge male *Nero di Parma* bigger than him. He made a rhinoceros horn and cape for it and watched it one dusk charging around the pen trying to shake it off. His aunt, unsure of what she was looking at screamed, dropping a huge cauldron of spaghetti she had come out from the kitchen to drain.

The pig got its own back by outmanoeuvring him next feed time, lifting him and the metal bucket against the electrified fence. Both squealed volubly. After a drubbing Ignatio didn't feel he deserved he responded sourly they were a semi-wild breed and should not be penned scheming by a kitchen door. The *status quo* remained tenuous for the rest of the pig's life.

His most recent passion was the idea of a Bornean Pygmy Elephant. Providing a fully-grown male with 200 kilograms of grasses, palm fruit and bananas every day would be his greatest challenge. It didn't take much working out what would happen to it on a regular Italian diet.

Ignatio wanted land enough with the house for a miniature working farm but discovered that getting land from a count was like pulling teeth. The purchase had been a secret because Ignatio realised he could only remain on the estate at the behest of his brother once title and property passed to him. Papa saw the problem and agreed to the deal, a 99-year lease. He also knew his eldest-born would need to be aware of such things and had first sought his agreement. This he would also keep quiet for the time being.

Italian law specifies equal inheritance between sons and Vespucci over many years had acquired land and property elsewhere sufficient to balance the worth of the estate. It would thus remain intact for the eldest and his family. Fair enough, he thought, regarding the separation of the château. A patch of land here, factory there and various apartments in his second son's portfolio, even if they were in Bergamo's highly desirable *Città alta* and on the sea front at Rimini, was not his idea of home either. It was also a better future arrangement for a second son than him being dumped on the Church.

What were to happen if there was no male heir and could the house be reserved for an eldest daughter and her husband if there was no second son, Vespucci had not got to grips with. Answers to complications like this might have to wait for a revolution, though the formidable Anna had her ideas on the subject.

Reaching the orchard, a soft wolf-whistle greeted Ignatio as he ducked beneath the remains of an old stone gateway at the upper limit of vine growth in the hills, his meeting place with Gabrielle. This they referred to as 1783 because of the date carved in the stone. Here Ignatio smiled the first real smile of the evening.

"Such a fine handsome man tonight!" Gabrielle cooed.

Ignatio did look the part with his rugged features and an impeccable white dress suit made for him by Armani. The warmth in Gabrielle's face disappeared momentarily as she touched her clothes. They were rags and could not be described as anything else.

It didn't matter to him except her discomfort about this in his company. The situation would change, he promised. Here was a girl who had no idea how pretty she was, a shepherd's daughter, the eldest of six in a desperately poor family, seventeen years old and ...

"... and you will always be my *pin-up.*" he said, developing her thoughts.

The gentle smile reappeared and she jumped up excitedly saying she had a gift for him. It was a shoulder bag for his food when out climbing, woven from wool she had gathered, washed, carded, dyed and spun herself. Ignatio was overcome. This girl knew all about wool and sheep and spent a good deal of her day in the hills making sure her family's main asset was safe. She was even guilty of wool-gathering thinking about him she once said.

His eyes closed involuntarily with the pleasure of her touch as she adjusted his cummerbund and bow tie. He did not speak, though she saw his sadness. He had been concerned about this milestone in their lives, him now twenty-one and their relationship so tenuous. It was nothing to do with responsibilities, his career in the family firm. It was more a crisis of confidence about their relationship, his purpose, his size ... things all young men have a crisis over sometime in their life.

Gabrielle knelt in front of him again, as she did frequently when they talked even though she was only a head or so taller.

"You came of age a long time ago!" she said, holding out her arms. She added, with a little grin, "Now it is time to be as big as you feel inside!"

Her face clouded over for a moment and he knew she wanted to say something else.

"I am so happy to be here to congratulate you and Tino, on your *ventunesimo compleanno!* If I may ask of my man now, please, please stop calling him *Smurf* or *Pulcinella* ... you don't mean it. It upsets me a little ... sorry ..."

Ignatio looked at his watch embarrassed. She might be his girl but she took no nonsense. It was time he got back to his party guests and for Gabrielle to return to the farm before her father stumbled in from the village inn. Once again he wanted to escort her over a lonely mountain, much of which she would have to run in darkness. All he really wanted on his birthday he told her sadly, was for her to be their guest of honour. Soon, he promised, soon.

She always blew a little kiss on departure, as a nymph might in a moonlit forest glade. This time from the vineyard she looked him up and down and gave a cheeky *riverenze,* a 'curtsy,' before disappearing into the night. Once more Ignatio lost a little of his soul.

.

Penny Lane goes to Italy

3/1

Early on the morning after the party Vespucci was motoring down the Bergamo-Milano road. Spring was well advanced on the plains of Lombardy. Traffic was heavy with people trawling the huge quantities of food and wine that would be consumed at family gatherings all over Italy the following day, *Giorno di Pasqua*, Easter Sunday. Vespucci was on his way to another meeting at the Milan textiles mill. The company needed to take action to keep creditors away from the gates a little longer. It was a desperate situation.

Pucci Moquette, especially its *Tappeto Volante di Italia*, the 'Magic Carpet of Italy' was a household name but the company had been in decline for years, as had heavy textile industries across Europe. Evasio's problem was the fashion and fad for cheaper floor coverings in materials such as bamboo and coir that needed little processing apart from nimble fingers.

The catch-phrase "carpets your grandchildren will be proud of" was now about as current as the well-known *detergente per tappeti* that for years cleaned "a big, big carpet for less than two hundred and fifty lira." Evasio was two years younger than Ferdinand but the stress of keeping the company afloat had finally pushed him, on his doctor's insistence, to cruising. His Easter would be spent around the Caribbean.

The meeting had been called by the works manager *Signor* Biffi. Ferdinand was chairing it in Evasio's absence and it was he once again who would be facing an angry mob in the yard. The workforce wanted some guarantees in the face of a new round of redundancies. Biffi and the office staff also wanted to know how the 'secret' talks with the Ministry of Labour on the future of Vespucci textiles were going.

He had new problems that week. Fifty per cent of immigrant workers in Italy were made up of Romanians, Albanians and

Moroccans and many of the factory's long-term employees had begun grumbling about them putting up with more than their fair share. They wanted to know why there were also *irregolares* on the factory floor when their own jobs were at risk. The old-timers had astutely observed if the *tappetti* went down it was likely the *pasticceria* and *pomodori* would go with it. They had grown up with the Pucci name and with a loyalty of sorts didn't want it to die before they did.

Everyone else at the villa that Saturday morning was concerned with a giant collective hangover. Lucciano had not slept in his bed. At ten he was still curled up in an old carriage in one of the outbuildings clutching a bottle of Fernet Branca for the morning. He had stayed up until four assisting the bar staff. Cook knew the scenario but could not find him.

Ignatio had locked his door and was not answering. Cook walked around the corridors to *Signorino* Clementino's bedroom, tutting all the way about bottles and glasses everywhere. It was too much, *Venerdi Santo* without a mention of Mass, then a big party, when her mama and sisters were in the house too. And where, she wanted to know, was Philipina?

The door to Clementino's bedroom was ajar and she demanded to know if he at least would be getting up for lunch. He rolled his head across his pillow, opened his eyes and shut them again, afraid they would fall out. His throbbing head and Cook's merciless voice receded and for a blissful moment he had a vision of mountains pink and soft, thrust up to a pale blue sky.

He tried hard to keep the image alive but his head and Cook's voice returned. He was not sure what she was saying but muttered *"si, si, grazie ..."* and was thankful it took only this to get rid of her.

She saw movement as she passed through the young master's bathroom. The room was his idea of Classical but was pure twaddle with a bath nestling in the wings of a giant plaster swan. It had taken him years to create and was impressive from the far end of the attic. Close-to it was clear a continuous battle was being fought to stop the creature from crumbling in on itself. Now there was someone in it wrapped in a *piumone.* She would be having words.

Ignatio was awake, lying on his four-poster with the shutters partly open. The woollen bag his *innamorata* had made was on the bed with him. The fresh air felt good on his face but the rest of him burned. He had been agonising most of the night about the situation with Gabrielle.

He had certainly grown bored with 'Rico, his bright green Quaker Parrot wailing bits of Puccini and Verdi arias it had learnt from the Victrola recordings of his namesake. The bird admired Donizetti too, Bergamo's own celebrated composer but would choose his most melancholic songs. When not singing forlornly it was sounding uncomfortably like Lucciano with a vocabulary colourful enough to make even visiting tradespeople wince.

Enrico Caruso, the greatest operatic tenor of the early Twentieth Century was a friend of Great-grandfather Vespucci. He brought back one of these intelligent, talkative birds from South America in 1901 as a present. The tradition of keeping one at the villa remained, all of them named 'Rico.

Great-grandfather talked often about his friend's ill-fated debut at Naples' *Teatro San Carlo.* Ignatio was full of admiration for the singer's stand against the custom of hiring *claqueurs* for their vigorous applause, non-stop *bravo! encore!* and glowing reviews. From a dirt poor background the young tenor was shocked at the concept of paid sweetening, *sucre* in French and never appeared there again.

Ignatio would have paid up. He had thought about taking some *claqueurs,* actually *claqueuse* if there was such a word, around with him jollying him along with something between cheerleading and adoration. He might have picked up some tips from his brother's theatrical friend, Fat-face Sophie but hardly ever talked to her. She was seldom without her clique of *claqueurs,* her *claquette.* They were more like flip-flops.

He had many good male friends in Bergamo but they did tower above him and often didn't give him manoeuvring room. Being higher up they were better at spotting girls and he was fed up with second-hand information on so important a pastime.

He once auditioned a group of town girls but they were not loud enough and his classic Maserati at the time, the little one, was not up to the job. He got rid of it, never again wanting the trauma of not very adult females whining in the back just because they were bent double. He didn't find it uncomfortable. They told him sourly he didn't make it with his sunglasses either.

His English friend, Tel, said three seasoned English *clubbers* would be as loud as ten Italian girls after a line of shots and big him up beyond his expectation, probably above their heads. Ignatio thought about it and realised after drinking like that they would be running him. He didn't like to ask what *SX Girls* were. His dictionary didn't have the word *sleb* in either.

Now he had no car except for a Trabbie awaiting strengthening after the two-litre engine shoe-horned in almost broke the car in two when he put his foot on the throttle. He had already fitted an 'Italian army' gearbox, those with one forward and five reverse gears, Tel's little joke. He had turned the body around and fitted a swivelling driver's seat. Once his passengers were inside he would swivel to the steering wheel on the parcel shelf and zoom off 'in reverse.' The instruments and switches, such as they were, remained on the original dashboard and he would call out to his passengers to switch lights on, indicate maybe and tell him how fast he was going.

It helped that the car already looked arse-about-face but he anticipated some technical problems, not least with the *Carabinieri* and when he was driving on his own. At this point he sighed. He wasn't able to take his girl out for drives in the countryside or visit friends as normal young men could so there was little point in a motor car anyway.

Cooking and climbing remained his best diversions. This was evident to those who knew his apartment on the top floor on the sunny side of the villa. He had a well-equipped laboratory in chrome and stainless steel that Cook was in awe of and to which she frequently alluded. It was only right for Pucci Pasticceria's Technical

Director, Ignatio reasoned, to have facilities fitting for the challenge of the role.

He had books about food microbiology and nutrition rather than recipes because he experimented rather than prepared dishes. Cook found this hard to fathom and said he should have a library with all that equipment. Along with "some experience," "his Mama's recipes" and "what's a poor woman like me supposed ..."

All around his actual bedroom were trophies and photographs of first climbs, by other climbers. An entire wall was taken up with a magnificent aerial photograph of the north face of the Eiger. He was obsessed with conquering the mountain after reading of the little Japanese guy, Maki, being the first to do it in 1921 by way of the Mittellegi Ridge and Gendarme. He didn't stop there, so to speak, becoming the first to climb Mount Alberta in the Rockies also. Size certainly did not matter here.

Ignatio had a detailed map and photographs of every part of the ascent and would lead a team of mini-skirted climbers from his All Frills Mountaineering Club. Never mind the first climbing of the North Face in the Winter of 1961, his first would be the one remembered.

Dominating his bedroom was a real-life mobile on the ceiling.

When he first saw pictures of the Schlumpf Brothers' house in Switzerland with a Bugatti in their living room, he wanted one as well. Papa baulked at the cost and he had to settle for a natty little post-war Topolino, the rare sports coupé version built under license in Germany, a Weinsberg Roadster. He was ten years old when it was delivered by Emil from St. Moritz and brought up the staircases in large pieces. This is where he learnt to drive it, on the top floor of the villa, albeit in first gear and reverse. It was his brother who noted he was learning how to get into tight corners but not necessarily how to get out of them.

Ignatio's next big mistake after stealing the limelight with his superior toy was to paint the roadster red and yellow. Clementino began calling him "Noddy." Ignatio countered with Mr. Plod. Their slanging reached the point where Clementino said the car had as much go as Clockwork Mouse. It was only when Ignatio took to slipping a blue cap with tinkling bell on his head and adopting a jaunty little walk when they were in public that his brother finally got bored with the taunt.

That was ten years earlier. The car was still in his bedroom, a little crumpled. It was suspended from the ceiling minus its engine with a life-size Noddy enjoying the ride under a plethora of silver stars. The engine had been sold, rather unsportingly he thought, to pay for the damage he had done to the villa's main gate.

Now at midday on his first day of adulthood he decided the only way he could approach Papa about Gabrielle was with a series of questions.

"Was he a mouse?" he would ask. He would refute this with one or two examples of how courageous he was. He would stand boldly in front of his papa and challenge him to give his reasons why Gabrielle was not good enough for him to marry. She was not of course, was what Papa would say.

He would then ask if there was any reason why he shouldn't fight him to see who the real *capo famiglia* was. Sliding deep under the covers at this point he could do nothing but shed a silent tear.

Then from the depths of his hopelessness and despair came an idea. He emerged from the bed sheets. It was simple. What he needed was advice. He would seek advice from the woman who knew everything, from a woman of whom even Papa was afraid, Cook.

He dressed quickly and strode through the upper corridors as though it were a summer morning and he hadn't a care in the world. Oh, such longings he endured as a teenager, such desires over female visitors he remembered, stopping by the carved door of one of the villa's many guest rooms. And how he had been treated as an object of curiosity, someone to pity, laugh at, be embarrassed by, stare at, fear, avoid, patronise and have his hand held so he didn't fall down the stairs.

He shuddered as he cast his mind back but told himself he had come of age, that now he would be positive about everything. If something had to be done he would live up to his fiery name and just do it and maybe get a continent named after him, as one of his ancestors had.

He plucked a primula from a bowl on a hallway table and as he stood fiddling to get the limp little flower into his buttonhole the door opened, a bleary-eyed female in her knickers greeted him cheerily *"ciao, Ignazio!"* and asked where the bathroom was. Mumbling, he pointed to the third door on the left and watched the girl with waist-length hair, her arm across her breasts, walk down the corridor. He had no idea who she was.

"So the *Signor* Ignatio has decided to get up this fine afternoon. And how is a poor woman like me supposed to ..."

"... If you don't mind, Cook," Ignatio interrupted, surprising himself with his masterful tone, "I'll have a *cappuccino* and roll on the patio."

Cook, to Ignatio's satisfaction, was speechless but on the patio he wondered if he should have snubbed her then when he was seeking advice. Perhaps he should wait until later. Then he remembered his resolution and decided he must speak while the going was good. There was no sign of Lucciano. The kitchen was his favourite haunt.

"Cook ..." he began more softly when she appeared with his breakfast.

Cook wiped her hands on her apron and smiled.

"What is it?" she coaxed. "What is it you want to ask?"

"I have a *compagna*, an *amica*," he began. "She is the most beautiful girl in the world. But somehow ... I don't think Papa will agree ... will agree to our marriage. I wondered what you thought ..."

Cook thought fast. There had been muttering about a Vespucci boy and one of the daughters of that no-good Farangio at Fóppolo up the valley, a rumour she had dismissed. But why not she thought as she looked upon a sad young man. It had to be the eldest girl Gabrielle. She was the lively one that kept that family together.

"I think only nice things when two people are in love," Cook responded. "Your Papa also, I have no doubt. It is just a matter of getting him used to the idea."

A huge weight lifted off Ignatio's shoulders. Sitting on the patio beyond the kitchen he looked at the mountains tinged pink and gold and capped in a delicate white, like that of Easter lace. The valley was soft in the afternoon sunlight and he could almost hear the wood anemones opening.

3/2

Easter Sunday is the one public holiday in the year when a good Italian pays attention to his family and friends. Vespucci was certainly born of this tradition and each year bought presents for a large number of his relatives. He did his share of food shopping too, having called in at his favourite shop in Bergamo old town's Via Colleoni on his way back from Milan. A large family lunch was the high point of the holiday and this year, Cook's and Lucciano's many relatives had stayed on after the boys' twenty-first to help in its preparation and with its eating.

The menfolk passed a boisterous Saturday evening in the village *trattoria*, returning late up the mountain road on foot, with lanterns and the goat. Cook and the other women who only got together at

Easter, made the most of their confinement in the kitchen on the Sunday morning. They chattered away, occasionally screeching with laughter as they drank wine and prepared food. The result was a magnificent eleven-course meal culminating with the *capretto delle nevi* roasted in olive oil, dry white wine, garlic, rosemary and seasoning. Roast kid is traditional Easter fare for Romans and for folk up in the mountains.

Keeping the Italian Christian respect for bread apparent, Cook first served a soup and *casatiello,* a savoury bread filled with cheese and tasty bits of meat for the Neapolitans among them. After *lasagne* and *capretto al forno* came the desserts, a huge range including the ultimate Easter treat *Pastiera Napoletana,* a sweet custard pie of wheat berries, ricotta cheese and candied peel in a lattice-topped pastry crust. Cook's Mama made her usual enormous *colomba* in the traditional shape of the dove of peace.

As always there were exquisitely-wrapped *uova di Pasqua* Vespucci placed around the house to satisfy the most determined stuffing of good Italian chocolate. The occasion was as ever, *Natale con I tuoi, Pasqua con chi vuol,* 'Christmas at home with your family, Easter with whoever you wish.' Before Christmas became commercial, the older folk reminisced, children loved Easter best because of the smells and tastes and decorated sweetmeats so deliciously tempting after interminable fasting.

Much later that evening after a lighter supper and dancing, Clementino and Ignatio left the villa in the Tino Dino for the drive to Anna's house in St. Moritz-Bad. Taking up most of the back seat with their bags and some equipment was one last sumptuous Easter egg containing many individual chocolates. It was a gift from Papa to his cousin. He knew she would admire it for a few days, then hand the chocolates out to the children in the street during the week, unless her son got them first.

The high passes were closed because of late snow and it was a good four-hour drive via Lake Como and Chiavenna. The journey could not be left until the following day. *Pasquetta*, 'Little Easter' is the first picnic day of the year and though a touch cold in the mountains for the traditional outdoor *tavolette*, every Italian car that has wheels on it is on the road.

Vespucci's problems with the workforce did not go away over Easter. On Thursday there was another ugly incident and mid-morning Friday he was again at the factory gates. This time he was confronted with a very surly workforce, a sombre Biffi and two cars from the Milan City police. Knowing they came out only if there was a body, Vespucci was concerned. It was the same troublemakers, Biffi told him, only this time they had knifed someone. Vespucci knew the men were concerned about their jobs but was convinced the undercurrent was political and dissent was being managed.

The following morning he flew to Rome and on to Naples for a meeting with his tomato growers. His suspicions were confirmed. Something was being stirred there too.

Returning late that Saturday night he retired wearily to the library with the supper Lucciano had left him. The day's mail brought further dismay. There was a note from his contact at the municipal tax office warning him of a planned visit by the tax inspectorate. Of more concern was the acidic article on the front page of the previous day's Il Sole about a foundering Vespucci empire.

He folded the pink pages of the business daily and activated the bar. It was at moments like this he missed his wife most. He treated himself to a good Scotch whisky offered a toast and undying love to his pearl, Margherita and decided she would have urged him to take up Lucciano's suggestion and 'phone Penny Lane in Liverpool again. Lucciano has a native wit she used to say, of the sort that controls half of America. She was of the same stock and understood these mysterious ways.

Ferdinand looked up the number of his sporting lady friend, his fencing partner at Oxford, Miss Lane for the second time that year. He toyed with the idea of telephoning her at home in Birkenhead, across the water from Liverpool, rather than at her office. You can ask a favour of an Italian any time but with the English there is the ritual to remember, the discretion, the hesitation, the *beating about the bush.*

He dialed Penny's direct line instead and was spared midnight apologies with the command *"Speak ... in an accent I can understand ..."* He would ring again first thing and fly to Liverpool at the lady's earliest convenience, that day if possible. Tax matters could wait. The recovery of the money owed by the Swiss bank was more pressing.

3/3

The brass plate inside a foyer of one of the imposing buildings that make up Liverpool's Albert Dock reads PENNY LANE AGENCY. Those who use its services refer to it as "Penny for Your Thoughts," or "Contact with Miss Lane ..." Its cut-and-thrust in a razor-edged world is legendary. Fencing is the passion of this company's CEO, a striking figure in the physical sense when kitted for competition. The Agency is also known for its discretion. A guitar features on its logo, demo tapes are played in the office. It has even been known to secure recording deals, one per decade on average.

Miss Lane was direct in conversation and humorous in her expression, as are Scousers in general, our Italian count was to learn. He liked the English words he had learned from her, clobber, ciggy and brekkie that had to be abandoned with more regular English-speaking clients around the world. On first introduction he marvelled at Miss Lane having an accent "just like a Beatle." He failed in that social encounter since Miss Lane had heard only this since starting her term at Somerville. It got worse with him losing every subsequent engagement on the gymnasium floor over the next three years.

If Penny's accent gave him trouble fresh on English soil, he was almost defeated by that of Mr. Lane at afternoon tea at the family's small estate on the other side of the river in "posher" Birkenhead. Primed to expect "flat cap and whippets" was no help whatsoever. At least he gleaned that afternoon Penny was christened after the street she was born in.

Penny's easing into the family business of health and beauty parlours did not live up to a feisty young daughter's expectations.

Soon breaking with family tradition and after a magical time in Germany, which is how she described the episode with a *Baader Meinhof* boyfriend, she was to inherit the family business. She was soon making radical changes. From her father's original aims of 'beautifying the beast' and 'soothing salvation' Penny Lane Agency now offered a range of services in the twilight area of political and social restructuring. It was transformation to take your breath away.

"How nice, Ferdinand!" Penny said as her old Italian friend was shown in to her office. "May I wish you a *feliz Pasqua* ..."

"And a happy Easter to you, Penny," Ferdinand replied, adding cautiously, "your Spanish is good ..."

"Oh, my apologies, *conte*. With my linguistic start in life, languages have never been my forte."

There was a moment's silence. Vespucci was almost sure Penny had read modern languages at Oxford but didn't pursue the point. He tried to thank her for the package delivered to the villa earlier in the year and it took only a glance to make him feel distinctly foreign. Their chat, he was reminded gently, would be over lunch.

"Do we still refer to that as 'scran?'" he asked beaming.

"With woollybacks and foreigners it is 'lunch'" she said, pinning her hair up and donning a tweed cap and matching tailored jacket. "And I apologise in advance for the Italian theme. It will certainly not be lunch as you know it."

More used to women with bright red lips, big shoulders and ostentatious jewellery at business meetings, Vespucci was charmed by this CEO's feminine, sporty look. Compensation for his weekly mis-matching he remembered, was the conciliatory smile and platinum blonde hair tumbling over her shoulders as she removed her fencing mask.

"And may I enquire after your mother?"

"She is well, thank you. I speak to her every day. She remembered this morning without prompting, the handsome Italian I brought home for tea. She thought at the time we made a good team .... you know how scheming mothers can be."

"That was until it was clear you were the better fencer. I recall the afternoon being a traumatic test of the Received Pronunciation my tutor had worked so hard on. Please tell your mother, of the tea and scones I have had around the world since, none compares with the ... spread ... she laid out that afternoon."

From the start of their hastily-arranged lunchtime meeting, even during pleasantries, Penny's disquiet was clear. Over pasta with a sauce that made him wince Vespucci brought the situation with the promissory note up-to-date, reminding Penny that capital and interest would only be paid out in the first week of August following notice of withdrawal a full twelve months before. Notice had been given but with four months to go, acknowledgement of the request was still not forthcoming.

Penny eyed the bread sticks in the jar between them and sipped the white wine served 'Italian style,' possibly, in a water glass. It was during the Autumn, Ferdinand went on, when his solicitors and accountant needed to refer to the original document, they knew the bank was stalling. They were unable to open his vault box. The new key and the family's amateurish escapade in February worked, in principle, he said proudly. The consequent non-possession of the document was now, with a looming deadline, a matter far darker than they could handle. Payment or legal redress without so much as a whiff of the original parchment was a non-starter.

A harassed young waiter appeared with a blue-veined cheese, asking in a terrible Italian accent if they would like. An unsmiling CEO said they liked the Italian theme to the lunch, even if the cheese was Stilton. When he had gone she commenced with her questions, asking firstly of Pucci liquidity. Vespucci hesitated. He was eyeing a *tiramisù* that was more like the trifles he occasionally had to dodge at college parties.

"Now is not the time to be shy over such things," she responded with an almost absent parrying of two *grissini* from the jar. "I have kings and princes admitting they are broke. If you don't tell me, my Reservations Department will."

"And no doubt send me the bill," Ferdinand added laconically. He assured the good lady that family honour was to the fore and they would meet their obligations.

She raised the count's eyebrows again by asking of the accuracy of the article in the previous Friday's Il Sole. Vespucci dismissed it bravely and she lapsed into silence. The casting of a Swiss bank's master key was a relatively inexpensive favour. Actually taking money from a bank was out of the question. Also not viable was turning over the bank to find a single document. Then the tiramisu, the restaurant's phoney version of it gave her an idea.

It was to Ferdinand's relief she agreed to assist further. She would make a return visit to Italy in early May to brief him personally. Operations would then be passed to her man Wilson. Indicating that the waiter put lunch on her account she suggested Wilson would follow up with two or three days at the estate before the end of June if the count insisted they as a family were to remain on the front line. Ferdinand, determined the family fought its own battles as far as possible and knowing the deadline was tight, accepted the responsibility for success rested with them.

It was on leaving the restaurant Penny complimented the count on the ingeniousness of the February plot, saying she could hardly have done better. Ferdinand, slipping back into his high-powered Italian shoes as she whistled for a cab, replied gravely he trusted the Agency was able to do rather better.

Penny allowed her old adversary the advantage and a handshake and smiles on the pavement indicated work had begun on the largest problem ever confronting the Vespucci family, its survival. He said how much he looked forward to her being his guest for tea at his modest estate in Lombardy and returned to Malpensa that afternoon a revived figure.

Penny Lane goes to Italy

4/1

The interior of the *contessa* Anna's home in St. Moritz-Bad is a big surprise after its modest exterior tucked away behind some shameful 1960s architecture and neon signage in the lake-side spa area. Many do not give the quarter a second look since old buildings, its architecture, is not the reason people are there. The *contessa's* house is, nevertheless, a Seventeenth-century winter *palazzo* built by her Italian husband's family. A winter retreat with its own *sorgente termale,* 'hot mineral spring,' in the magnificent setting of the Upper Engadin was certainly not a Nineteenth-century invention.

The *palazzo*, a modest *eredità*, an *annualità* from the family's Lombardy estate and the courtesy title *contessa* was left to Anna on her husband's death ten years earlier. Using these assets she set up an office in her home and began buying up family-owned land and property in Switzerland and Italy as it became available through the family's growing financial embarrassment. As a young woman she had no say in what was obviously mismanaged family finances. Now she was making a point.

The return on some of these historic and run-down assets was an eye-opener to the *contessa's* side of the family, including Ferdinand. He was full of admiration for her drive and ambition. She openly admitted it was her business to keep the *chic* of the village alive. It was shameless because San Maurizio's best-kept secret was that it had no charm whatsoever, except the high prices many find comfort in. Her smile she said, was a fixed one.

Used to their elegant home, the boys tried not to cringe at the neo-geology featured in the interior restoration of the *palazzo.* The retaining of many historic features including a recently uncovered passageway to the hot spring was to be admired. Roman masonry and bronze plumbing had been restored.

It was the *contessa's* taste in the new areas of the house they thought retro to the point of troglodytic. Part of the lower ground area, for example, was sculpted like a subterranean cave with stalagmites and stalactites of a pure white crystalline material brought in by the sack load. Hidden among softly-lit rock pools were various seats, bookcases, bars and flat screens with romping areas before them. One of the toilets featured a bowl that exuded thunder and lightning effects when flushed. In one of the shower rooms, turning the water on prompted vibration and the sound of stampeding elephants a little too close for comfort.

More restful were continuous grotto sound effects such as dripping water, frequent whooshing and what Clementino was sure was the occasional cry for help from a human voice far down the system.

All water features led to the grotto's main pool. The warm bubbling water was lit from below. There were falls and flumes everywhere. The mineral water issuing from the lowest area of the house at 40 degrees Celsius, carbonated and rich in iron was once drunk as a cure for anaemia. Now, after it had been temperature-controlled, they just bathed in it. Good for blood pressure problems, it left Anna's skin feeling as soft as a baby's with an accompanying sense of well-being. It also heated her house and domestic hot water.

The view from the third floor was mostly free of the Stalinesque blocks that characterise ski resorts. The boys were in adjoining bedroom suites and could see and hear along the lake shore the fairground they liked, its coloured lights, shrill organ, whiz bangs and squeals that kept the Summer evenings vibrant long into the night.

Sharing a bathroom and erratic mealtimes caused some grumbling, though they liked getting their own breakfast. Not that they were spoilt of course, like all other young Italian males. The countess would frequently tell them, as family they knew where the kitchen was. *Yourself ...* or *self,* she would say quaintly in English, rather than "help yourself" or "self-service."

She would often gravitate to the kitchen in the early hours in an exquisite silk or satin chemise drooling over the contents of the refrigerators. She prepared a lunch and evening meal for her guests, her son and chauffeur Emil, sometimes working through the night. She loved the sensuality of food, she said but giving in to it was masochism.

Clementino, also a night owl, never saw her with anything more than a single grape or cube of cheese or solitary prawn without a dressing. The Roman glass wine goblet she drank water from had an iridescent sheen of blue, yellow and green that added subtle colouring to her face. She seemed blissfully unaware she too could be drooled over.

She was a beautiful woman and they were sorry with their lack of success in persuading Papa to visit her more often, to court her. Here was a wasted *bellezza*. She was younger than Papa and they would surely appreciate each other. Soon, Clementino and Ignatio agreed, they would begin a campaign to get *Cupido* riding high.

Their ongoing entertainment over Easter was the countess's son Fazio. He would normally have been in Italy with relatives over the holiday but the previous year the crowds and fireworks in Florence, particularly the exploding cart, the *Scoppio del Carro*, had frightened him. He said his relatives were "too religious" anyway, so *Mama* kept him home.

With chocolate around his mouth and on his fingers all weekend he was obviously in his element in Switzerland. Here were chocolates, chocolate bars, bunnies, biscuits, cakes, candy and eggs in coloured foil brought by thousands of 'cuckoos' as though early Christianity had depended on chocolate consumption.

There was a *Zwänzgerle* in town where adults threw coins of twenty *Rappen*, or *centimes* with gusto trying to get them to stick in chocolate eggs. Knowing they must keep the eggs as cold as possible, Fazio and his friends coined it in. The growing lad was also partial to *Osterfladen* and once scoffed an entire cake in front of them while his mother was not looking.

He had become immensely smug having passed them in height by one centimetre, and more horizontally, that year. He would not get away with it. He was eleven and along with chocolate, he was interested in football, girl bands and in learning to play the accordion. He loved his *fisarmonica* and was very upset one evening, after he had been a bit cheeky, to discover it had been tampered with, making his Ode to Joy sound more like wind being expelled.

They could always wind him up about a particular football star they referred to as Davide Peckham which they thought was his real name. On one occasion, not knowing his real talent lay in marketing, they asked if he would not be taken more seriously with a little tattooing perhaps, to mark him out from the crowd.

Clementino, never without his water colours, ridiculously covered the young Peckham's visible torso on the poster in his room with tribal graffiti. Fazio burst into tears. He stopped wearing his slippers that looked like football boots after this. He also wanted the AstroTurf on his bedroom floor removed.

The pop girl posters sported more subtle additional illustration that also caused the boy to run off to find his mother. His big crush was Roberta from Lollipop. She mysteriously became Robert with cropped hair. Clementino gave him/her a Mussolini MVSN cap. *Il Duce's* looked like a black girl's pubic hair permed to one side so he emphasised the vaginal crease on Robert's. Fazio had a crush on a girl who looked exactly like his mother, was Clementino's convoluted point.

Then there was Emil. He showed little restraint in his being mad about the boy. Fazio, unsure of details but adept at attention-seeking was awfully close to having the point driven home. His mother drifted around, seemingly oblivious to what she had no idea was sexual tension. Emil being also amused by the boy meant she was spared continuous biting and she liked hearing her podgy little son was beautiful. It was a situation so obviously fraught, family and even visitors puzzled over it.

Clementino and Ignatio's attitude to head-in-the-clouds parenting, with due respect to their father, was to get on with life anyway. A century earlier Fazio might have been known as a 'sickly' child who had to be pandered to, though one robust enough when out of sight of his parents.

The weather during this refreshingly different week was also a great tonic. The boys enjoyed the fixed-rope climb to the summit of Piz Trovat at over 3,100 metres. Their glacier walk was cancelled because of low cloud but magnanimously they challenged Fazio to keep up with them on the high-rope course at Pontresina. The Dino would have been a squeeze even for three little guys so, also magnanimously, Emil took them in the big car. He complained throughout the fifteen-minute drive about no-one wanting to sit next to him.

The boy was exhausted by the end of the afternoon and admitted respectfully his old half-cousins beat him roundly on every section.

"Serves him right!" observed Ignatio who thought the boy was spending too much time in his room playing silly console games with friends while snacking. The great outdoors, just beyond the door, was out of sight but within reach. He wasn't called Fazio for nothing.

The boy tried one last bit of one-upmanship with the help of a school friend but Ignatio turned the allegiance with a bag of marbles and pack of girlie playing cards. Fazio became the butt end of a fiendish practical joke involving laughing gas, melted chocolate, squirting cream and the school friend videoing a clip promised for YouTube exposure. They would have no more trouble from *Signorino Blobby*.

"Who wants to be twenty-one anyway!" Ignatio observed on the drive back to Bergamo. They hadn't had so much fun in a long time.

He was mostly quiet, vowing in silence that on his next trip to Switzerland Gabrielle, Lella, would be with him. They would travel from Tirano to St. Moritz on the Bernina Express for the spectacular views from the highest railway line in the Alps. They would walk and climb together. She had it in her to be a good climber. He had seen her on a rock face in a summer dress without equipment, fearless, erotic ...

She would love Engadin's first day of March spectacle known by its Romansh name *Chalandamarz*. The village boys are busy from dawn with cow bells, whips and general whooping in blue tops and red woolly hats to chase away the winter. Their reward is plenty of sweets. Lella's treat would be the spa at Heilbad. She had no idea what a spa was. With her beside him it wouldn't matter that a special plastic block was brought to the Jacuzzi so he didn't disappear beneath the bubbles.

4/2

At the beginning of May, shortly after their return from Switzerland, Penny Lane visited the villa with their plans for the retrieval of Vespucci property from the Zürich bank. It was late in the evening when Clementino went down to the sitting room to wish Papa and the Liverpool Lady a good night. Ferdinand relieved the red, yellow and blue pantalooned Papal Guardsman by the fireplace of his halberd to move a log and get a better blaze.

"So now, My Dear Penny, we are alone," he said after a supper that had lingered longer than he expected. "In the past there would have been a log boy. Now it is Lucciano, though tonight, he is off. I can tend the fire and am able to guide you to the kitchen should you start feeling peckish."

"It has been a while since I, well, stuffed myself, with such good pasta, salami and hams and that beautiful Aosta Valley cheese." Penny admitted, undoing one more button of her waistcoat.

A ten-course lunch with wines had floored her. After meetings that morning in Liverpool and London it was actually her breakfast and she had been obliged to rest for part of the afternoon. Another large spread and three wines that evening had also been a challenge. Soup *ossobuco* with a classic *risotto alla milanese.* Cook was very particular about the quality of the Arborio rice she used and came to ask if it was to their guest's satisfaction.

The evening meal was topped by a sample of Pucci's own special *panettone* with a sweetened brandied cream and trolley of Cook's inimitable *pasticceria* Penny could only admire while sipping a last coffee of the day. She kept to herself that it was with regret, when she was obliged to drink mineral water and eat salad for the sake of her figure, that men clearly had the better deal.

"To think my father, when he ran out of ammo, resorted to

throwing salami and petrol-filled wine bottles at the enemy on the push North through Lombardy." Penny said, slipping into a masculine after-dinner mode, ignoring the admiring looks from the man opposite her.

"That was a while back if you're talking of the *Tedesci*," Vespucci replied.

"It wasn't the salami and Molotov Cocktails that saw them off. His battalion had a vanguard of at least a hundred farmers with pitchforks, sickles and Tommy Guns wanting the Germans off their land and out of the country. Brave they were too, with the way they, the SS in particular, were punishing civilians in villages on their retreat late in 1944."

She fell silent trying to remember the year Italy became a member of the European Economic Union, at how quickly it had recovered from the war, then remembered the country was a founding member. She recalled being cornered in a Rome bar in the early 1980s after making the big mistake of uttering the words "Margaret Thatcher" and "Common Agricultural Policy" in the same sentence.

"But, to the task in hand," she began, taking a file from her attache case and a Sobranie Black Russian from her bag, inviting Ferdinand with a smile to light it for her. "This promissory note problem is an interesting one Ferdinand. The name of Saltzmann's bank, the Sweinchencommerzbank, puzzled us too. My staff translate this as Saltzmann's Little Commercial Pig Bank."

"Perhaps Saltzmann's Commercial Piglet Bank is better business English?"

Penny leaned back in her armchair grinning.

"The Saltzmanns were originally Bavarian pig farmers," she went on, "according to their own archive material. An old Jewish family, their first bank in the Zurich Canton in the early Nineteenth Century provided funding for the pig-rearing community. It became a general commercial bank, later private and now incorporated. The pig reference remains."

"I don't know of a religion that is not interested in money, even if not *kosher*. And perhaps we should read 'turncoat' rather than

Marrano into 'Christian' Saltzmann?" Vespucci suggested pouring his guest a glass of promised vintage amber nectar.

"And the abbreviation 'SS Commerz' on its internal documents? Hardly *Steuerverwaltung Staatsanwaltschaft,*" Penny asked, putting her glass down and taking a sheet of paper from the file.

"Or even *Steuerrekurskommission Sachverständige,*" Vespucci added cynically.

"And certainly not *Schlichtungsverfahren Schätzungs-kommissions!*"

"So you did study Modern Languages at Somerville!"

"Er, yes … but I'm reading from a list of suggestions provided by my Research Department being just too clever, as with *Schwangerenberatung Sachverständige …*"

"… Pregnancy Counselling Experts?" Ferdinand translated.

They burst out laughing.

"And if they weren't that bit too clever, you would be making changes!"

Penny turned to the hearth, a smile and blazing logs lighting her face. The light played beautifully through platinum blonde hair and the rich hues of the Armagnac. She took a sip and mumbled approval. Vespucci sighed. It was a treat for them both, a 1923 Jean Cavé. He would like to have offered his guest more during her stay but realized he might have embarrassed her just a little already.

Penny was reflecting on there being little her client needed to be briefed on regarding banking in Switzerland. There was an association between the Vespucci family, the German language and Swiss banks as long as there had been banks in that part of the world. He was not aware that the Saltzmann Sweinchencommerzbank was one of several banks criticised in the 1999 Volcker Commission Audit for questionable conduct regarding assets likely belonging to victims of Nazi practices. An estimated 50,000 accounts were opened in Switzerland during twelve years of the Nazi regime by people concerned with the security of their assets. Only recently, she confirmed, had tardiness in restitution to surviving family members been addressed.

"Over the same period," she went on, "the Swiss National Bank also took in assets knowing it was loot. The government's Banking Act of 1934 that codified bank secrecy was ostensibly to stop pressure from Nazi authorities wanting information on the assets of families they regarded as enemies of the German State. It was also protecting some very dodgy dealing."

"It is not far-fetched to think that a bank on the Swiss side working secretly with the Nazis would be in a very good position indeed as long as discretion was maintained. This very German bank in 1934 was suddenly very Swiss in 1935, according to changes in directorship and statutes. The ability to access private vault boxes at a time when gold, gems, deeds, bonds, paintings, were a safer investment than cash deposits would have given the Nazis a very sharp edge. And terms must have been lucrative for your father to risk the Vespucci family finances in such uncertain times?"

She grinned adding it was quite something young Clementino had stumbled on during his night in the vault. She stressed that similar audacity was needed to ensure the return of the assets. On top of this, eight hundred million Swiss francs was the net income of the largest of the cantonal banks. For the smaller Saltzmann bank to raise such a sum of money in the wake of a global banking crisis might mean its downfall.

"I view it with less emotion," Vespucci responded grimly. "It is us, or them."

"And so we come to the people behind your problems."

On the cover of the folder Penny handed the count was printed *Freude Bringend!* Vespucci opened it and flicked over the first pages before tutting,

"How shameless a euphemistic name for a Neo-Nazi organization, 'Bringing Joy!' And how worrying that such an organization can flourish today."

"And behind that bland corporate name, as you will read, is a hard-core organization with the name *Stalhelm*. It is headquartered in an office in a private language and communications college near Würzburg. Their extension is an answer phone to us outsiders but the power of this organization must not be underestimated. It has substantial assets, has a membership of thousands around the world, is administered by a handful of staff and is controlled by six men. Six men and a dream, a ghost maybe. It is real, bitter-sweet in its ideals and thuggish as required."

Penny rose from her chair and asked if she might dispose of her cigarette end in the fire.

"No cloak-and-dagger stuff here and nothing to do with the paramilitary force known as *Der Stalhelm* that existed between 1918 and 1935," she resumed. "The newer *Stalhelm* was born in the 1950s. Its creation was more through a dragging up once more of German Romanticism, I would say. This time more sober. It has never sanctioned black leather-clad skinheads or overt use of Nazi symbolism."

"Having said this, our *Stalhelm* actually came about on January 30th, 1933, the day Adolph Hitler became Chancellor of Germany."

Ferdinand looked at her carefully.

"Its founder is Baron B. Rothenfelder. You'll see he worked his way up from Hitler Youth, through medical school, to junior aide on the *Führer's* medical staff in '44 and '45."

Penny went on to say it didn't need his Research Department to be clever buggers in spotting Fascist sympathies in the Saltzmann bank, in its inclination, its business dealings, its personnel and its social and cultural programmes. She would leave the folder about this particular Neo-Nazi organization and its bank for Vespucci to read.

"So now to our plans. There are two ways we can approach this problem of the missing millions. We could use an associate that specialises in global money transfer. Monies belonging to you, once retrieved, would be placed somewhere as safe as is possible, without others watching and providing our associates are able to do … what they do. Their non-returnable fee, payable in advance, is high and their commission if successful, is in the region of forty per cent of the retrieved asset."

Vespucci flinched.

"The alternative is more taxing, er, more of a gamble perhaps but rather less expensive," Penny went on. "We use a bargaining tool."

"As in bargaining chips?"

"We must relieve the bank of something of theirs that will concentrate their minds on releasing money they will exchange for the said goods. Let us then hope they are able to suck back money as easily as they funnel it offshore."

Vespucci leaned back in his chair and ran his hand through his hair.

"Not another Enigma machine, or signed photo of Eva, or gold bars stamped with the *Reichsadler* and swastika. It would have to be the real diaries of Adolph Hitler, his ashes ..."

"How about his DNA, evidence of progeny, of his living out his old age in Brazil where he was known locally as the Old German?"

Vespucci opened his eyes wide.

"Documentary evidence exists for these things and such important paperwork is likely to be held ..."

"... in a bank ... their bank ..."

"How are you disposed to spending Christmas in Lombardy?" Vespucci asked his guest as Lucciano was putting her case in the car early the following morning. "After our meeting I believe our celebrations this year will be more up-beat, I think you say, than they have been for a while!"

"Very kind, *conte*," Penny said pinning up her hair and accepting Lucciano's offer of a cap and scarf against the brisk mountain air.

"The year's end is the time when we as a family celebrate our good fortune, our privileges. We personally deliver a *paniere* to every family on the estate on Christmas morning," Vespucci said proudly. "But you know all about strong traditions in, Liverpool?"

Penny laughed. "If we let it, it becomes haggis, Hogmanay and that wee Andy fellow that carried Christmas for decades! But it is not so good at my end. The boyfriend will be, er, elsewhere and I will be doing my usual, visiting my reprobate brother up in Edinburgh ..."

"Yes, I seem to remember ..."

" ... things which are best forgotten ..." she said with a sideways glance. "His housekeeper does the equivalent of your Cook on Christmas Eve. She comes armed with one of her splendid haggises and a bottle of cask strength Scotch, sixty per cent alcohol, from a Lowlands distillery of which her brother is a director. It is an annual kindness but I have to admit to using it to set fire to the logs in the hearth, before my brother can drink it. And the haggis, that usually dies in the Rayburn."

"But all is not lost?"

"Oh, indeed not. The day will start with one of his *Atholl Brose* breakfasts, oats with cream and honey soaked overnight with a measure of his favourite thirty-five year-old malt. We have lunch in the nearby hotel. Then it is back to work for me. But this year I am thinking of something different, Christmas by a pool in Barbados, with my girlfriends. We all agreed recently Christmas is just a pain in the ..."

"... much more fun, letting your hair down in the Caribbean!" It was Ferdinand's turn to interrupt. "I will make a point of remembering where you are with a toast of our version of a Caribbean Christmas punch."

Penny Lane goes to Italy

5/1

Ascension Day, *Christi Himmelfahrt,* that year was celebrated in Germany in the middle of May. It was also the date of the annual *Freude Bringend!* rally. Two thousand people were enjoying the get-together in the immaculate grounds of a private language college on a pleasant Spring afternoon in Würzburg in Northern Bavaria. Here were former comrades-at-arms, family and friends, students and a Middle Class hugely interested in consolidating the revival of German greatness. A greatness built up over the previous half-century through prudence, hard work and a perceived superior ability. All were familiar with *nationalsozialistisch* and *neonazistisch* ideals. Many knew the ideology behind this annual rally was upheld and promoted by the *Stalhelm.*

The principal of both organizations was Baron B. Rothenfelder. In his late eighties he was still CEO of a pharmaceutical company with manufacturing facilities in Switzerland, Germany and several South American countries. Controversy had surrounded him all his life over his Nazi interest and his firm's trading in dubious drug markets. Journalists had been on the scent since the 1960s. Some had paid a high price and recent hounds were very cautious indeed.

Rothenfelder was nine years old when he saw Hitler spot-lit in the window of the presidential palace in Berlin on the eve of his inauguration. The adulation whipped up that day fully demonstrated Joseph Goebbels' talent as writer, editor, public speaker, propagandist and campaign manager for Hitler over three years of elections.

To a boy brought up with solid Christian values he was overcome with the messianism he had learned about with awe in the Bible. Confirmation that he would dedicate his life to the cause came ten years later on hearing the words *"für apokalypse, lesen Blitzkrieg"* uttered by a senior member of Hitler's cabinet. He knew the *Führer* in the last two years of his life, attending him many times in the New Chancellery, Berghof and Wolf's Lair.

There was a special treat at that year's rally after the baron's candlelit address at dusk. A dynamic group addressing some bold ideas for the future and calling itself *Die Goldkinder* was making its first appearance. Rothenfelder would be introducing these 'Gold-Children' after the Grimm's fairy tale, gratified by seeing their brightest sons and daughters, also a grandson and granddaughter, coming to the fore.

Listening intently to their leader as his talk got under way were senior *Stalhelm* members Hartsburger and Lispman. Rothenfelder already had that year's gathering in his hand with an almost unassuming announcement that of an estimated 60,000 books acquired by the *Führer* during his lifetime, a handful had been in his safekeeping since 1944. Lispman had not heard this before. Hartsburger suggested they slip off for a beer and sausage. Lispman held back. Part of Rothenfelder's firm grip on the organization was his ability to surprise.

As he was pondering this, Rothenfelder, on a stage set between silver birch trees, opened and held high a small leather-bound volume. He pointed out to a spellbound audience a passage marked with three stripes pencilled by the *Führer* himself. He put the book down carefully on his lectern and almost whispered into his microphone,

"I will read the passage to you in a moment. First, I want to tell you something about the inspiration for Speer's Theory of Ruin Value and how it relates to our world-wide cause today ..."

"... today, private grounds in Würzburg," Hartsburger muttered in the marquee as one of the attractively mature *dienstmagd* brought sausage, beer and a big smile, "tomorrow Hirschgarten in Nymphenburg Park, right back where we started ..."

Lispman offered up his *stein* and told his comrade not to be morose. There was vitality in the movement he said, munching on a sausage. The RAF's firestorm that obliterated the city in 1945 would not be forgotten, as Londoners would not forget *der Blitz*. American military units had gone, Würzburg's *Hofbräu* beers were the best, reunification had been achieved. It was only a matter of time.

He was heartened to see his colleague loosen up on his second jug of beer and hearing the periodic applause from people around the park, many now holding candles to their bosom. The local *rosswürste, sauerkraut, erdäpfelsalat, bier* and even the maid with her well-rounded *Ostfränkisch* dialect were icons of the German way of life. Lispman's family prospered during the 1930s and 1940s and this college was one of three his family owned in Germany and Austria. Times had never not been good, he reminded himself.

The two days following the rally had a different tenor. They were set aside for meetings with *Stalhelm* members and guests from around the world. By ten o'clock wives and family members were conspicuous by their absence, the college was returning to a holiday period calm. Groundsmen, gardeners and security would be finished by midday and the gates once again closed.

The solemn and private piecing together of a standard issue M1935 army helmet by the *Stalhelm's* six senior members had taken place at dawn. This helmet had been cut into seven pieces and was assembled on a leather interior that rested permanently on a wooden head. When assembled its decals were clearly visible, the black, white and red shield on the right side and the insignia of black shield and silver *Reichsadler* on the left holding the swastika in its talons. These were a feature of the helmet until 1939 when they were toned down or removed because they were like beacons in combat.

Six men held a piece each. The seventh piece and person were missing. The six *extant*, including Rothenfelder were:

Gottfried Hartsburger, accountant, paymaster and fund-raiser for the organization; Gerhart Lispman who was in charge of marketing, public relations and media manipulation; Franz Schumacher, a specialist in work force dissent who worked with right-wing and left-wing organizations to this end; Otto Vogler, who was responsible for the world-wide recruiting of agents to serve the cause and Hans Kleper, the most sinister of the Inner Circle. University professor, historian, author and homosexual, Kleper was an expert in National

Socialism and SS and *Gestapo* interrogation techniques.

The missing piece left a large hole in the upper front of the helmet. Here German romanticism gave way to the Jewish messianism Hitler abhorred. As with the prophet Elijah having a place laid for him and a door left ajar at the supper of Passover because his appearance heralded Christ's at the Second Coming, so this piece would one day be in place signalling the return of the *Führer*.

The *Stalhelm* was thereby, six men and their Guiding Light dedicated to a spectacular resurgence of Neo-Nazism amongst the world's youth. It was a grand and costly ideal they had committed their lives and much of their personal wealth to. It was unfortunate on the first morning of meetings that being hung over was a less attractive part of rally ritual.

Rothenfelder warned Hartsburger at breakfast they should not be side-tracked by trifles at their 09.00 meeting, particularly with talk of *Stalhelm* and Vespucci bank accounts. He reminded his colleague that during the financial austerity of the late 1930s the *Führer* had the foresight to give Speer an open cheque book for the construction of the Reich Chancellery. The money materialised, more than 90 million *Reichsmark,* the equivalent of a billion dollars today and the benefits of such a seat of power in the following years was incalculable. He told Hartsburger he considered the matter of their overdraft dealt with.

Regarding the second item for discussion after breakfast, the Italian Affair, as the Vespucci loan had become known, Rothenfelder beckoned Schumacher over to their table. He was well aware of the ongoing industrial action putting the Pucci companies under pressure and wanted an update from the divisional head.

"They will sink without trace," Schumacher affirmed, unsure of whether to put his breakfast tray on the table, "the repayment will become a moot point. Remember we are dealing with midgets ... oh, excuse me, midget companies!"

No one else was amused. Hartsburger gave short shrift to the suggestion the matter of the loan would disappear with the Pucci companies. Creditors and banking commissions would be there, picking over the carrion.

Rothenfelder made another swift decision.

"As agreed the last time we convened, the Vespucci assets are not to be released. We will ride it. They are Italian and they will not get their act together on the matter. The authorities have plenty to be occupied with on the Berlusconi witch hunt. Our meeting is deferred, gentlemen. Half an hour in the park among the crocuses and daffodils in this sunshine will be a more agreeable way to start the day. A better way of clearing a head for a ten o'clock start, when we are scheduled to have them blown off again by our *Goldkinder Wunderwuzzi!*"

There was silence around the table until Rothenfelder added, "and, gentlemen, how remiss of me not asking how your wives are, those I did not have the pleasure of meeting this year ..."

5/2

A few days after Penny's visit to the Vespucci villa the Agency's Italian-speaker, Wilson, arrived for what he referred to as the first rehearsal of the Zürich "gig." Penny's 'secret weapon' was wearing a white linen suit and Panama hat and approved heartily of the beautifully-tended vineyards, cherry trees laden with fruit and end-of-May weather south of the Alps. Hale and hearty, Vespucci and his sons warmed to him. Vespucci knew what a British public school education could do to a man. His two sons only saw a confident front, huge energy and big smile, not a prat.

The van Wilson had driven from Belgium was parked by Lucciano in the main outbuilding. He had brought some climbing equipment with him not knowing the extent of the younger Vespucci's expertise on buildings or how much kit they had. He was impressed the boys knew what all of it was for, including Edelweiss O-Flex about which they asked immediately of the need for indoor climbing rope.

After Vespucci's apology for half a lunch, that is, only six courses which Wilson packed away without difficulty, maps, drawings and print-outs were spread across the larger dining room table. Wilson said he was known to repeat himself because the data associated with their gigs was invariably complex. He did repeat everything that afternoon, in Italian and his audience of three was grateful. They complimented him on his mastery of the Italian language.

"I have relatives near Genoa alive today who spoke their *Genovese* dialect exclusively until the 1960s," Vespucci said. "It is nice to hear again that Portuguese, North African, inflection. It is tuneful, even soulful to our ears."

"As you can hear, my father was a Genovese. He went to London after the war and built up an *ice-a-cream* business," Wilson said grinning. "His English didn't improve much so this little *monello* was speaking like a Ligurian native by the time he was five. I didn't realise it was not Italian until the first time I came here with the school. Then I had to do some homework."

Late the following morning after looking through all of their climbing equipment Wilson watched the boys scale the villa, cross the roof and abseil the other side. He seemed satisfied and as he sat back with the Pucci tomato juice aperitif offered by Lucciano, opening his eyes wide at his first sip, he said they would run through the brief again after lunch, this time with him as their audience.

When he bade farewell to his hosts that afternoon the Vespuccis almost crumpled in their seats in the study. The count chuckled.

"So there we have it my sons. At the start of the August holiday, Saturday the first, Herman unwittingly lets the robbers into the bank after Saltzmann's habitual late-night departure. Herman is held hostage. The rear entry is accessed by Team One. There is some acting by several masked men on the lower floor of the bank for the benefit of Herman and his television monitors. The use of cutting equipment is started and aborted and card games commence above and below with some bogus exchanges on walkie-talkies. This is a charade covering you two accessing Saltzmann's office through the chimney. You find your way to the rear of the vaults, retrieve ... whatever ... and make your escape by dawn."

Clementino and Ignatio liked the ease with which their father had just effected the robbery of a Swiss bank. What they should also have expected was him getting up suddenly from behind his desk and blurting out,

"But I can't permit it. I cannot put my sons, the family name at risk, at being caught, imprisoned, shot at even ..."

"Papa," Clementino began almost wearily, "we have discussed this *ad nauseam*. We have one chance and there is every reason to believe ..."

He was about to say a possible court appearance, prison even and the publicity over a missing or retrieved promissory note should still lead to success, when his brother excused himself, left the study and vomited in the hallway.

Their training across the roof of the villa and largest outbuildings began next morning. They had five weeks in which to practice and almost every structure on the estate was climbed at all hours. In between they chipped away at a brick wall dividing fruit and vegetable gardens. This was the closest Wilson could find to the bricks of the bank's chimney.

Then began emergency rescue drill along with careful study of surveillance video clips and photographs. One of Wilson's team had walked around much of the bank with an array of cameras on him like a Google Earth van, except his were miniature. The resulting footage provided a 3D snapshot of the interior. Areas not accessed on his 'getting lost' in the building were Saltzmann's office because it was locked and the ladies' toilets because ladies were in it.

Ignatio had one diversion he could have done without on the roof of the château he had just bought. His normally voluble brother said absolutely nothing on putting his boot through some well-oxidised copper sheeting on rotten laths. This was very suspicious. One of them knew more than the other was letting on.

When Wilson returned early in July for a final rehearsal and to talk to the rest of the household about security in the weeks after the headline act, the boys announced they were ready. They had settled on their preferred equipment. It related mostly to weight. They simply could not carry 'adult' packs. Wilson picked painstakingly through it then watched them in action across the château roof.

"Seconds must be clipped off the time it takes you to pack, unpack, put on and take off equipment, especially the jump suits. And yes, you will have some of your size on the day," he said over the walkie-talkie. "You must get better at everything one-handed. We would only be able to assist on the roof in an emergency, remembering we're far too big and clumsy to get down the chimney as you guys can!"

Back on the ground he told them bluntly they were still bantering too much.

"Anyone would think we were twins, with adjacent rooms and ..."

"... My point exactly," Wilson responded without smiling. "The monsters we are dealing with, the Swiss banking system and the organization behind Saltzmann will be slumbering while we are rooting in their jaws. All of us will have to be quick. Banter, bickering and buggering about slows action dramatically. And while I'm lecturing, do not forget the message of the Second World War 'Idle Chatter' posters. It's not quite *chiacchiericcio* but you know what I mean from your British comic collection."

That Wilson could climb was obvious and that didn't mean him getting on and off his high horse, Ignatio quipped quietly to his brother. He didn't get out much on the end of a rope, he had admitted, the last time being on the Old Man of Hoy. He had written his name in the log book in the cairn on the summit four times, none of the climbs having been done in Spring or Summer because there were usually too many people on the stack. Next year, he said, four of them were taking on the Matterhorn.

"We're just keen amateurs, so we'll scoot up the easy way by the north-east face and Hörnli Ridge!"

The brothers glanced at each other.

5/3

As soon as Wilson left the villa, tension surfaced again. It was not surprising considering the boys were not criminals yet they would shortly be attempting a robbery professionals would baulk at. Excused of all duties relating to company business, partly because all Pucci business was on an alarming down-turn, Ignatio and Clementino took to their quarters and began brooding.

Over the years, taunting and sniping had sometimes continued for weeks. Clementino's ability as a painter was a favourite target, as was Ignatio's interest in school work. They took an obvious form, as allusion to the tiny figure striking the hour of a steeple clock, Jack o' the Clock. This would be countered with Jack Brag or Little Jack Horner or a very sharp Pinocchio. One day Ignatio remarked it was the hand of Little Jack Frost that put the finishing touches to his brother's painting. Clementino fell into the trap and blurted out his brother meant Jack Sprat.

When their knowledge of English nursery rhyme characters petered out, for they had shared the same books in English as children, they started on Collodi's tale. "Jiminy Cricket" was traded for "Blue Fairy" and "Honest John" for "Donkey."

It was at this point their father demanded to know what they were muttering through mealtimes. Being tediously parental he remarked they should be more respectful to each other regarding their names.

"Tino is acceptable," he said smartly, "Igno is not."

The taunts ceased, until Clementino re-discovered Brewer's Dictionary of Phrase and Fable.

In their perceived problem of surviving in a world where 'size matters' Clementino was at one with his brother. It kept them on speaking terms at least, through their teenage years. They were treading the same path, they understood each other's reticence on certain things, their anger over others and daydreaming about the rest. They also shared each other's triumphs.

Most recently Ignatio had created a range of perfect miniature pastries for the firm. Clementino's initial reaction had been to sneer at his brother's 'pixie bites.' It wasn't long before he admitted they were good, with its ingeniously flavoured pastry. Their American wholesale outlets thought so too but did insist on referring to the range as 'party food,' sometimes even 'finger food, Italian style.'

Clementino knew the hours his brother had put into perfecting this *antipasto da intenditori*, "*hors d'œuvre* for connoisseurs." He occasionally risked climbing over the roof from his side of the villa to peek at what he was up to in his fancy kitchen.

Clementino's apartment was completely different. He had decorated the panels in the bedroom with cherubs mimicking those in other parts of the house, though his were wearing little headphones from the pocket tape-recorders that were once all the rage.

He wanted a Borgia's bed for his sixteenth birthday in the hope that an uninhibited girlfriend would help him explore its possibilities. He settled for a circular one to match the bedroom windows through which there was always something going on, from the maid practicing with her lipstick below left, to spectacular thunderstorms over the Valte on the upper far right.

His main business and leisure pursuit was drawing and painting and his studio took up the rest of the apartment. A whole section of the gable roof of the north-west wing of the villa had been replaced with double-glazing and fitted with electronic blinds facilitating near-perfect lighting for painting. The studio was light, airy and Spartan. The roof timbers were visible and the supporting walls almost bare.

And so too, one afternoon in mid-July after Wilson's last briefing, was Sophie. Clementino had placed his dearest friend on an alabaster pedestal in the skimpiest toga he could find. She was holding a Greek urn strung up to the ceiling but her arms ached nevertheless and she made it known frequently he was taking longer than usual on his first sketches.

Also irritating Clementino was the small electric fire casting a red glow on this maiden's otherwise proverbial milk-white thighs. He changed it for a warm air fan. This wafted her toga and really was a distraction but he decided he could put up with it. He really wanted her in his bath for a Leida and the Swan picture but was unable to bring himself to ask because of how she would have to pose. He was exploring Classical themes because that type of illustration, with cheekier cherubs and lustier maidens, would soon be returning to the Pucci product range.

The most chary aspect of his drawing session that afternoon was Sophie's two fellow actors parodying adoring fans. While he was trying to paint, they were *ad libbing* a play. The eldest, a lady of about thirty with cropped hair, red lips and fishnet stockings could have come off a Bertolt Brecht set. She could not take her eyes off Sophie. The youngest wasn't taking the theatrics too seriously. She had ingested something that made her giggle inanely and eventually pass out.

All three sparred with each other without touching, speaking in highly mannered terms. Sophie, a thwarted dramatist as well as model responded to them through Clementino, the fourth wall, their baffled audience of one. Here was a painful example of Brecht's *Verfremdungseffekt*, his 'estrangement effect.' Clementino was uncomfortable. He had long ago been dismissed for being unable to add anything intelligent to this, or for that matter, Pirandello's device of metatheatre introduced to an unsuspecting public in his 1921 play *Sei Personaggi in Cerca d'Autore*, 'Six Characters in Search of an Author.'

His ill-considered comment he was but a humble artist was met with a broadside of the achievements of other 'humble' artists. Why, he was asked, was he not painting them with the virility of Klimt, Schiele or Picasso? Cut down to size, so to speak, he thought of retaliating and naming the ladies after the three Sirens. Already out of his depth he knew his fate would be one of drowning in a sea of insults.

While Clementino was struggling with his afternoon of art, theatre and lesbianism, Ignatio was warming himself on the sunny side of the house. He was sitting on his roof terrace flicking through his diary counting the days to when he would next be meeting Gabrielle. It was usually a Wednesday or Saturday evening, once or twice a month. This time it had been six weeks.

These infrequent, stressful trysts had become sadly normal after three years when Lella was almost fifteen years old and he eighteen. That winter had been the worst. Heavy snow meant they met once only in three months. She had wanted to ski to see him but he forbad this as far too dangerous. It would have taken her half the night. Instead he risked taking the Range Rover over the pass closed by snow and a daylight meeting in public fraught with danger.

They had another painful reminder of the unsatisfactory situation at the end of January during a brief thaw. They turned a corner in Bergamo and came face to face but had to walk away from each other. She was with her father and two brothers who hadn't noticed him. He was hidden in a crowd of several friends. Gabrielle knew something bad was about to happen moments before. She had passed a nun and was unable to transfer the bad luck by touching someone else with the words "your nun."

Ignatio ignored the superstition. He would remember forever what she was wearing, from scuffed red shoes to a red spotted headscarf knotted under her chin. Even though the encounter was but one second it hurt them both.

How Ignatio hated Gabrielle's father with his comments two years before about him being a *folletto*. Gabrielle had cried over it. It came about when she first mentioned, with extreme caution, how nice one of the Vespucci sons had been to her when she slipped on an icy hairpin bend in the village and fell across the road with her shopping in front of his car. He had been quick enough to haul her out of the way before another car skidded into the back of his.

"Goblins one, goblins all ..." reverberated around the valley kept buoyant by his drinking and the laughter of his cronies.

Gabrielle suffered other verbal abuse. One day, her father said, his eldest daughter would marry a real man, someone who knew what toil in the fields was all about, who would know how to keep her in order ...

Ignatio was soon teasing her about her ruby red shoes until he realised they were her only outdoor footwear, apart from Wellington boots. She wore them around the hills with the sheep, when visiting relatives and when shopping in Bergamo. He was ashamed of his indiscretion.

He thought of enquiring at the Vatican about what the Pope did with his old red shoes then decided when they were married he would instruct Maestro Stefanelli at Novara to make a pair of Moroccan leather shoes for her, presuming he could fit shoes to Cinderellas as well as to Popes.

The distance between the Vespucci villa and Gabrielle's farm in a straight line over a mountain, ravine, irrigation canal, meadow and pine forest was eleven kilometres. They had two other meeting places apart from the stone archway near the villa. One was near Gabrielle's village, the other at about the halfway point. They alternated these three places to share a considerable walking and sometimes running distance and in Lella's case, risk at being found out she was leaving the house after dark.

Their mid-way meeting place was at the bottom of a steep valley along which an irrigation channel had been constructed. Very little water flowed through the system even during snowmelt and it was falling in to disrepair. Carved in the white stone of the sluice gates was the date by which they referred to it, 1894.

Their favourite meeting place was about two kilometres from Gabrielle's house on a little-used pass high in the forest and one of the routes they took to see each other. It was the end of two derelict houses with a barn. Uninhabited since the 1930s there was no-one left in the village who

75

could remember the families the properties belonged to. The land around had reverted to scrub and was only kept down by the local goatherd and Gabrielle sometimes, driving their flocks through. The faded enamel plaque over 'their' door showed it to be 187b.

It was their favourite hideaway because the upper floor, from which there was an escape to the barn loft, was dry and warm. Several layers of pantiles kept out sun, rain and snow. The shutters facing the mountains opened and closed. On the other side there was a hole in the wall looking down the track that led to the village. Heavy sacking covered it so no one could see the light of their candles after dark.

Here, they talked and laughed and teased, gazing at each other in a world of their own for an hour or so. They danced too when it was raining hard or an often strong *favonio* was blowing and there was less risk of them being heard. Their music in the sitting room came from a wind-up gramophone with a large horn. The records in the chest it rested on were broken but between them they got together a new collection. The gramophone was enjoying a revival, albeit with a pillow reducing its output to a squeak.

It was here Ignatio brought things for Gabrielle to taste when he wanted her opinion on a *torta, pasticcino* or *biscotto* his team was working on. He discovered she was an accomplished cook with things she brought him. There was no nonsense from her, from a palate that could not condone products being passed as cake in the *supermercati.* She baked for the family using good ingredients, most of it from their own land. He was impressed.

Most important to Ignatio was that he had managed to launch a *biscotto* named after her at the start of the year. He had not actually created it, though no one involved in its development knew this. It was Gabrielle's grandmother's recipe. He had even contrived Gabrielle's signature as the biscuit's logo. His brother had done a very nice job unwittingly adapting the script.

It was one of Ignatio's finest moments, showing his girl the prototype biscuit and packaging. She was so proud on realizing how clever her man was and how important he must be to Pucci products. She said they were perfect, except for the taste but was polite in her suggestions on how it could be improved. When Ignatio saw her the following month armed with a new packet her smile showed he, the production team, had just about got it right.

"Much better," she said, "but you still need better flour. Whatever you're using is too chalky, too white. You need tastier eggs and absolutely no *bicarbonato di ammonio.* The cinnamon taste would be more subtle if you kept it with the sugar in air-tight storage."

Now Ignatio was really impressed but he didn't go into costings. He did know he was committed to the family firm whatever happened between him and his brother and that he would not be doing it without Gabrielle. Her keen interest had inspired him to make an innovative, stylish projection of a new range of *artigianale* cakes and biscuits to be introduced over the next five years. He was bubbling with enthusiasm and ideas for it, many of which were Gabrielle's.

On an earthier level erotic dreams about his little friend continued. He was twenty-one years old and she now seventeen. They kissed and cuddled but no further was he allowed. It was not that she didn't want to, she said sadly, throwing her arms around him. It could not be then, or there at any of their meeting places.

He had to respect this and after almost three years it was so trying, so wearing, despite being a delicious torment. The frustration was doing neither of them any good. More than once he thought it would be just his luck she wasn't actually interested in sex.

To keep his mind off the imminent Zürich heist, bickering with his brother and to avoid having to tell one more *bugia innocente*, Ignatio had been working on a surprise. Gabrielle loved the evenings when he mimed to their records perfecting his performances to the point of them being cabaret acts. His shows usually featured forgotten operatic tenors but there were lovely recordings of the old crooners, Gene Austin, Al Jolson and Bing Crosby. The rare Caruso 78s, dozens of them given to Great-grandfather by the maestro himself, Ignatio decided he could not risk borrowing.

Lucciano was very knowledgeable about the Caruso collection at the villa, as befitting an archivist. He recalled simpler times when listening to the records, when no one had any money, there was little work and life crawled along through endless summers. It was pure nostalgia, he said. He was a pretty good baritone in his day, Cook affirmed proudly. He would sing at gatherings, sometimes in the *piazzas* in Naples, often with a tenor friend to collect a few lira and buy some food or a glass of wine if they were in favour.

The recordings had the opposite effect on Ignatio. The power of Caruso's voice, his expression and ability to hit a high C in a performance that would keep an audience on the edge of its seat opened flood gates for him. If he could have expressed himself in song to such a sublime degree he would have done so with as much fire, as much power, in the most elaborate of costumes. Instead he just sobbed.

Lucciano's latest find after gleaning the villa's unused attic was a 1932 recording of Paul Robeson singing Ol' Man River with the Paul Whiteman Orchestra. It was a good addition to the collection he said to Ignatio, though he had no idea where the Younger was stashing the records. Ignatio had perfected miming to it with a hat and cane routine more appropriate perhaps for an Al Jolson rendition.

It was midnight on a sultry Wednesday night at the end of July when he arrived at 187b. Gabrielle was waiting at the doorway in darkness with a glass in her hand. She had put wine in it for him, she said, her eyes sparkling. She didn't know what it was because it came from a plastic flagon but it was the one her father liked best. Once again, still unaware Ignatio would shortly be involved in a bank robbery in Switzerland, she detected a pensive mood. He brightened up showing her the new record, an oversize hat and cane and promised a performance that night that would defy description.

He began by standing on a soap box on the dusty boarded floor. His acting was amazing, right through to his struggling with his breath control considering he was miming to a giant who must have had lungs like tractor wheel inner tubes. Kneeling on the floor in front of him she laughed and laughed until the tears rolled down her cheeks at her *Picci* with such a deep booming voice.

She actually laughed so much she wet herself. Her hand went to her mouth in embarrassment but she had to tell Ignatio because he would know as soon as she stood up. As gallant as she could have wished for, he set about lighting a fire in the rusty old stove so she could dry her dress and knickers on the string over it fixed on opposite walls. There was plenty of straw about and wood he could break with his hands. He checked that smoke would blow away from the village. He was then asked politely to go into the next room.

He had another worst-twenty-minutes-of-his-life scenario. He had to make himself count to one hundred while gripping a chair, to stop himself peeking through the crack in the door. Beneath her dress and cardigan she wore only a short vest. It was either cotton or jersey, she said, depending on the season.

It was bad enough knowing she did not wear a *reggiseno* and was not shy in telling him other girlie things. He loved this but bra or no bra he occasionally fantasized over what it was like to be full height and feel a girl's breasts against his chest, or abdomen. He wondered if Gabrielle sometimes cuddled him from being on her knees because she had realised this.

One definite advantage of being short was that his face was generally at breast level. A cleavage, with a touch of Chanel perhaps, was divine. When really lucky, a breast might brush his cheek to be followed by an apologetic giggle. By far the most stimulating was colliding with Gabrielle, so soft, so natural. He was sure, with her smile she did this also to please him.

He could hardly look at her on frosty nights if her cardigan came open and he saw the shape of her *capezzoli* through her vest, dark, exquisite. His agony that summer night was greater even than this, or contriving to follow her up the steep staircase at 187b, for which he had not forgiven himself. That was when they first dared to enter the old house on a night neither of them would forget, for entirely different reasons. What would *San Valentino*, renowned for his chastity, have done he asked himself, apart from suffer?

His *adorata* was now stripped to her vest. He could not look. She was so trusting he just could not do it. He had reached fifty when she called out to say the fire was nice and hot now and doing the trick. Then she screamed.

Ignatio knew why. He smelt burning at the same instant. He burst back into the room just as she grabbed the sacking from the window, then her dress, clutching them to her front. To his amazement, panic over-rode sex and a glimpse of her bare thigh to her waist. Acrid black smoke was puthering from holes in the ceiling around where the stove pipe disappeared. There was nothing in the room he could use to smother the fire in the stove, certainly not the sacking. They were in big trouble.

That was just the beginning of a very trying night that featured a half-dressed teenage girl, half the village and two fire crews concerned about the surrounding forest. How they escaped from this conflagration and he got Lella home unseen with a fire lighting up half the valley, he did not know.

They were cut and bruised from having crawled through scrub and tumbled down a forested mountainside in the dark, like goats they remarked later without humour. Sadly, 187b, their gramophone records, record player and furniture, their little hideaway was no longer. But Ignatio was a big step closer to a more mature decision about their future.

Penny Lane goes to Italy

6/1

At the end of July Papa returned to the villa once again in silence from a meeting in Milan. This one had been with his accountant, a firm of auditors and Evasio's bank manager. He was probably too busy with all this, Clementino thought, to be concerned about a robbery two days hence they still didn't know was going ahead.

Confirmation came that evening with Wilson speeding down the drive in a van with Zürich plates followed by an unsmiling woman in a nice little sports car with Bergamo plates. She had a scarf around her head and shoulders and big sunglasses. She was introduced as "My Colleague."

She didn't waste any time on pleasantries apart from shaking hands with all three Vespuccis saying she looked forward to working with them. She opened the boot of the Alfa and lifted out two large and obviously heavy holdalls. Both Clementino and Ignatio went to assist but were told politely she could manage.

"My Colleague," Wilson began, "is ex-Services!"

"… yes, thank you, Wilson. Let's just get the stuff transferred," she said in an accent even stronger than Miss Lane's.

"The last addition to our kit, some builders' tools," Wilson said turning to the count. "We have at last secured our preferred option, a contract for internal work on the house five along from the bank. We said we wanted to make a start at the holiday weekend and take advantage of easier parking for the unloading of materials. Rendezvous with us in a similar van is at the picnic area outside Zürich tomorrow night as arranged. The car is for your two guys. We'll take their gear with us and be on our way. I do apologise for the flying visit."

"No time for …"

"… very kind, sir, but my colleague's military timetable is in force."

He glanced over to the van, its engine running. 'My Colleague' had changed into overalls and baseball cap and was in the driver's seat tapping co-ordinates into a mean-looking GPS unit. He showed the younger Vespuccis the car's documents and a small suitcase containing shoes, two neat little grey suits with tails and two top hats. No, it wasn't formal bank robbery attire he said, countering Ignatio. They had been briefed that a wedding was their reason for entering Switzerland that weekend should they be asked at the frontier.

"Everything is in hand, it would seem," Vespucci said, "so I would like to bid you all the very best of luck."

It was seven on Saturday morning when My Colleague brought coffee and what could be breakfast into the bare room in which Ignatio and his brother had spent the night in sleeping bags. The large hold-alls in which they had come into the building had gone and their gear was lined up against the wall.

"Did you have a good night?" she asked with the first smile they had seen from her. She didn't wait for a reply. She opened the curtain a fraction and reported it was sunny and the street deserted. She noted they were rested. They had been sleeping in their bags for two weeks, enjoying being up on their roof under the stars.

"There are seven of us in the building now. Wilson will remain here as Control. Myself and three others are Team One, the business. We are also your backup. You two are Team Two. Feel free to move about but keep away from the curtain-less windows and the skylight. The buildings opposite are higher than us. We'll probably be playing cards downstairs on and off this morning and making some half-hearted drilling and banging noises, until grub at twelve hundred. It'll be a long day for you two guys, so rest."

Ignatio, drawn to the smell of decent coffee was idly unwrapping the greaseproof paper packet next to it.

"What ees grub?"

"Oh, I'm sorry, *i-o non parli-amo* a word of Italian. Erm, I can get Wilson up here."

"No, ees okay! I speaka good English," Ignatio responded. He saw his brother glowering at him and rephrased the sentence, in Queen's English.

"Thank you, ma'am, we understand you perfectly."

My Colleague left the room chuckling.

The reason they had not commenced roof-crawling that Friday evening was because of Saltzmann invariably spending at least half of every Saturday in his bank. It might not have been the case on the August holiday weekend but they were being cautious. The first of August, a Monday that year, is Swiss National Day, *Schweizer Bundesfeier.* Banks are not open at weekends so there were three straight days in which nothing would be open. Saltzmann and his wife would be visiting her parents in St. Gallen, an hour's drive away, on Sunday or Monday.

It was about ten that Saturday evening when Wilson's walkie-talkie flashed. He inserted his earpiece.

"Okay! We have accessed the bank at ground floor level with our Saltzmann lookalike returning suddenly and having the door opened for him," he reported to Clementino and Ignatio. "Herman is trussed up like a Thanksgiving Turkey. They'll leave the monitors on long enough for him to see equipment being brought in at the rear of the building. A lot more play-acting will be going on down there. For now it's go for you guys!"

He pushed the skylight open, hauled himself onto the red tiles, peered around in the darkness and signalled for the gear to be passed up.

"Last reminder," he whispered, "first light is 03.47. Being on the roof dodgy after this. Watch your footing and keep below the crest. Good luck, gentlemen!"

6/2

Zürich is slow at any weekend and absolutely dead during the August holiday. At eleven that Saturday evening there was not a sound to be heard anywhere in the commercial district. It was a warm night and perfectly still, except for some feverish activity in and above one of its banks. Clementino stopped what he was doing to look down at the street lit up by a passing car. He couldn't see it even though the roof was steep. It turned towards the lake that was black except for some reflected light from the shoreline. Moments later all was quiet again.

Both Clementino and Ignatio roped themselves to the bank's main chimney stack for a breather. It had taken a creditable twenty minutes to chisel out the first brick. If the operation was to fail, Clementino thought, it would be here. It was like, well, like confronting a brick wall.

No such luck as finding a loose pot. In any case, there was a gas fire in Saltzmann's office and a flue pipe would make it too much of a squeeze, even for them. The stack had been re-pointed recently but mortar coming away in their fingers showed the standard of work to be the same as that of roofers the world over.

Clementino changed from a Frenchman's tool to a lead hammer and cold chisel, then the more usual old screwdriver to remove the mortar. Ignatio assured him the tapping and scraping was inaudible beyond twenty metres. By eleven-thirty they had broken through into the flue and could feel an updraught. With renewed energy it took only minutes to make a hole big enough for them to squeeze inside.

Clementino squatted on the pantiles, sweating from the exertion. Ignatio had also been working continuously, spreading debris over the roof tiles. He lined the bricks neatly on the slope over the rear of the building. It was partly so that they would tumble into the yard rather than the street if dislodged. It was also important they were hidden from the buildings opposite.

After a few minutes' break, Clementino wired the grappling iron to the corner of the chimney and fed the line down the flue. He called for a time check and was aghast at seeing his brother shake his watch a couple of times and put it to his ear with a pained expression. It was another one new for the occasion, a Tissot that was a bit big for his wrist. It told him everything including compass direction, temperature and barometric pressure at a touch. The compass had come into its own on the way to Zürich where Italian road signing had failed completely and mountains had blocked the GPS signal.

"Just kidding!" Ignatio whispered. "It's 23:34 and 56 seconds!"

Clementino said nothing. He had regained the moral high ground after a queasy moment thinking about what they were doing up there and was now smiling at the thought 'in for a penny ...'

Inside the flue Ignatio found everything much harder than he had envisaged. Soot and tar smarted his eyes, he could barely control his descent and his bespoke 'onesie' that even covered his boots was restricting his movement. At least the balaclava part was a form of mask that made breathing easier. Fabia, their cousin in fashion had made them and warned they would have to go with mixed colours because she only had samples of the required stretch fabric. They were practical, even *di moda*, she said, even if they looked like *arlecchini*.

Five metres down, the flue divided. He had to take the left side looking down and to the front of the building and was very concerned with how narrow it was judging by how little he could move his boot around. He then went hot and cold realising he had turned several times and couldn't remember which way he was facing.

He pulled a handkerchief from one of the suit's zip pockets and with some difficulty wiped soot from his eyes, torch and watch. The compass facility gave him his orientation.

"Temperature's gone up three degrees ... barometric pressure's up. It'll be nice later ..." he said into the low-range kiddie's walkie-talkie from the same pocket.

"Bloody ..." came the verbal rather than audio response from not far above him, "... switch the bloody thing off."

Locating the correct flue had been a major concern. One suggestion had been for Team One to make some white smoke in Saltzmann's office fireplace. They fell about laughing at the thought of it signalling a new leader for this particular large and wealthy organization. It was eventually sorted by a careful comparing of the interior of the almost identical building in which their operation was based.

Ignatio doggedly descended the narrower shaft. When his feet met the fireplace throat he braced himself alongside the gas fire's flue pipe and slackened the rope. It needed only the dimmest beam from his torch to show how easily he could get stuck and the night's first serious thoughts of giving up crossed his mind. Mercifully, claustrophobia was not a problem. He was not an escapologist either. So pleased was he at seeing a relatively cavernous fireplace his concentration slipped as he wriggled through and he strained his back.

He unclipped himself from the line and sat in a pile of soft soot breathing hard, highly conscious of the noise he was making including coughing and sneezing. He was in the correct fireplace. He could see through a hole in the corner of the fireback a slash of red carpet and enormous desk, one bigger even than Papa's. Banking was obviously the business to be in. The street lamp beyond the window was confirmation it was Saltzmann's office. More cheerful now he ignored the likelihood of abuse from his brother and whispered into his Donald Duck handset "the Duckling has landed."

The fireback moved readily outwards as far as an antique gas fire that also slid squeaking across the hearth. Only a few more centimetres and he would be in the room. He shut his eyes when he heard hissing. He pushed a little more and knew as the hissing became rampant he had ruptured a gas pipe. The sickly sweet smell caught his nostrils. In an all-out effort he forced his way through, saw where the pipe had broken and was relieved he was able to turn the gas off from just within the fireplace. There was a lever above it which he lifted for no other reason than curiosity.

After laying out a clean plastic sheet, removing his romper suit and listening at the door he reported all was clear. He said nothing about the big surprise. It was Clementino who reasoned that access to the rear of the vaults would be in a private location, away from security cameras and public areas. It could only be Saltzmann's office, the main room on that floor. He could put a Do Not Disturb notice up, lock the door and get on with some 'extra' business.

"Elementary, my dear Wilson!" was his comment, to the delight

of the Englishman, though Holmes never said this. It was Ignatio's job to find this passageway entrance before his brother lowered any gear into the room. When Ignatio radioed him to drop the three bags containing tools, extra rope and other bits and pieces, his brother didn't question him.

Ignatio warned him about the narrow throat. He wanted to tell his brother to forget the tedious "little" Father Christmas line he spouted every year after a few drinks but he should be able to work out how dumb it sounded after an actual chimney drop. When he did appear entirely soot-blackened except for the whites of his eyes, Ignatio was unable to resist a quip about a Father Christmas for piccaninnies. He met a stare such as came with only the worst of his brother's moods.

"Let's just get on with it. Jump suits into a polythene bag, latex gloves, boot covers, the way down to the vault ..."

To which Ignatio responded with a deft touch of his foot. It was Clementino's turn to spin around in the half-light at the click and movement in the wall beside the fireplace.

"Swine," he said, realising his brother had discovered a secret opening, "I'll put you on my gold bag handout list."

"How come ..."

"... because as fast as I put people on the list, I cross them off ..."

Inside the cubby-hole was the top of a narrow iron-rung ladder that descended about six metres. Taking the minimum of equipment they discovered two further ledges and ladders within the walls. They touched bottom on the third level, a concrete floor in a narrow corridor with rough brickwork on one side and the rusted steel wall of the main vault on the other. As Ignatio had ascertained in February the wall was set with levers at regular intervals. It was a voyeur's fantasy, one he intended to indulge in, when his brother's back was turned.

Miss Lane had said that with global concern over tax abuse and Swiss banks under continuing pressure to divulge information about accounts, more of people's wealth might be converted to something they could put 'under the mattress.' Boxes remained, for the time being, completely private to the client.

They reckoned there were two hundred levers on the main wall. The passageway went around the corner where there were probably another hundred. Their first task however, was to retrieve Vespucci family material from this dodgy bank. It would also confirm 'Vespucci Was Here.'

Ignatio held the lamp while Clementino counted along and up and raised the lever. The heavy spring-loaded steel end with rubber edging lifted. They pulled everything out and packed it into polythene zip folders.

"Bingo, not," muttered Clementino seeing the promissory note was still missing from the deed box. "Time now to get ugly."

"Uglier than Nazis?"

"When we've had lunch, yes."

"Er, that's up on Saltzmann's desk ..."

"... bloody ... and we don't have time to climb up and back down."

They had less than three hours in which to find what they were actually charged with seeking, prime Nazi paraphernalia. His brother had already opened two more boxes and Clementino thought it best they were systematic in marking those they had purged. An equally tidy Ignatio agreed and rummaging in his brother's pack pulled out some lippy. He held it high in the dim light, his eyes shining.

"And what, may I ask ..."

"Camouflage, Nerd."

"Pink?" Ignatio asked, hoping it was the maid's lipstick.

Clementino grabbed it from his brother's hand.

"The tube is pink, Deviant. It's the normal translucent stuff to prevent chapped lips. We'll have to use that. Or there is another marked 'camouflage paint.' And about negative banter ..."

He didn't finish his sentence. Both of them froze on hearing laughter permeating the walls from somewhere within the bank. It was not, they agreed, ghosts through history having had a jolly good time in that particular hole.

Unbeknown to these two operating at the level of the city sewer,

Wilson's four colleagues inside the bank had untied Herman and allowed a little party to go ahead. The laughter was currently over Herman losing his trousers to one of the ladies in a round of Strip-Poker. Herman was wearing a posing pouch that looked like an elephant's head and trunk and swore he knew it was because they would be coming in.

Ladies, because the lone Team One member guarding Herman while the other three were playing cards by the vault entrance, was unnerved by two women and a man looking at him via the street camera, ringing the front door bell. He asked a still very nervous Herman for an explanation. Herman spluttered it was a special night, his birthday. His sister had brought two friends for a little celebration. They knew the boss had long gone and if they weren't let in they would be very suspicious. His sister's boyfriend was in admin at the city's police station.

Team One had done its work for the night, about thirty seconds' worth. This had included making a mark on the vault's circular steel door with a thermic lance. It would be, Boss Lady had said, "as easy as cutting in to tiramisu." None of them knew what that was but hadn't liked to ask. By midnight when the front doorbell rang, their gear, extinguishers, fire suits, oxygen and oxy-acetylene cylinders was packed away again and they were waiting for the two Little Guys to do their bit elsewhere.

The lower basement area was too confined a space in which to continue with a source of heat blowing molten metal and muck everywhere at 800 degrees Celsius. It was the excuse for the raid being aborted. Team Leader looked around on arrival and reduced the original three minutes of use of a thermic lance, to thirty seconds, a showing willing that included kicking plenty of sand about.

With flammable material everywhere, particularly polished wood well within the ten-metre danger zone in an oxygen-rich environment without ventilation, longer would have been very dangerous. Once the initial smoke and dirt had cleared, a quiet game of cards and some snoozing made it one of the easier jobs Wilson had dropped on his regular group of squaddies. They were relaxed enough to try cajoling My Colleague into making some tea and laugh when she told them to bugger off.

It was Wilson at Control five doors along who decided the three people waiting furtively outside the bank should be let in. There was no reason why the team shouldn't have a laugh upstairs two at a time while the 'robbery' continued below. The dummying was to keep the real accessing of the bank for Nazi stuff from public knowledge. A party might even help.

The door was opened by a trembling Herman. His sister saw this straight away and was about to ask what was wrong when they were hustled upstairs in darkness to the security office by masked men.

"So what's in the bag, Doll!" Team Leader asked, removing his balaclava. "Something for a party? We wouldn't want to spoil Herman's party!"

The sister's friend eyed muscular Team Leader in black leather from top to toe his eyes twinkling. The others looked pretty dishy too, hardly a ruthless gang.

"How about *schnapps und* strip-poker!" she responded in the kind of English he liked to hear, especially in a lilting Frankish German with a big smile. "If ve vin, ve take all ze money in ze bank. If ve lose, ve be generous and take only half!"

This would be one Saturday night these party-goers, along with most of Switzerland and Southern Germany, would not forget.

For the next hour down in the bilge, tiredness and hunger were forgotten as Clementino and Ignatio continued lifting levers and pulling out the contents of the boxes. On the whole there was remarkably little in the way of treasure. Sometimes there was a chortle or low whistle and the floor would look like a corner of Aladdin's Cave. It was usually because of *cartamoneta*, wads of it like it was going out of fashion. There were also *perle*, bags of *diamanti* and other coloured stones cut and *grezzo*, gold nuggets, gold dust which they had never seen and smaller items such as watches, paintings, ivory, pottery, stamps and coins.

Clementino had a careful look at an exquisite set of Indian miniatures marked 'from the court of the last Mogul Emperor, Bahadur Shah II, 1857.' In the same cubby-hole were several pieces of jade in a bag marked 'Boxer Uprising, 1901.' He knew these could be more valuable than the equivalent weight in diamonds.

Most common were papers, locked tin deed boxes and jewellery, all of which they ignored. Their brief was to collect anything that could be construed as a bargaining tool, in particular items relating to the *Fuhrer's* person. Everything else would be forgotten, almost.

The set of pornographic pictures Ignatio waved under his brother's nose was in the almost category. One of the snaps showed the very elegant naked lady wearing a rather splendid crown and gripping a large golden ball between her thighs, ecstatic in queenship he guessed.

It took them an hour to reach the five bigger vaults at ground level at the far end of the wall they had started from.

"Housey-housey!" Clementino exclaimed more convincingly, lifting a pile of documents out onto the concrete. "Just these five vaults and the tin boxes if we can open them. Put all the other stuff back carefully. It's obvious in hindsight they would keep the bigger boxes for themselves."

"All of it? Folding stuff, gold watches, black pearls? There's a diamond here as big as my ..."

Clementino took a deep breath but didn't need to speak.

Ignatio thought of secretly swallowing four little beauties from a velvet drawstring bag bulging with sparklers. Surely the owner would not miss them? Two could be made into earrings for his girl and two would make matching cufflinks. Maybe two more could ...

He got no further on his dare on realising he would have to come clean with Gabrielle with how he had smuggled them out of the bank. Unable to stop giggling over this and the possibility of them disappearing down the toilet led to him being swiped and the bag put back sulkily from where it came.

When Ignatio returned to see what his brother was poring over he whispered,

"The American Eagle!"

"No, Igno, it is the *Hoheitszeichen,* the national symbol of the Third Reich, the *Reichsadler.* We have before us *mein dummkopf,* archive documents with signatures of some well-known personalities. Having brushed up on my German for the event, like you didn't, these look mighty interesting. Campaign maps, too, including one for Britain!"

"And pin-ups," Ignatio interrupted on seeing a stylish Verichrome portrait of an actressy type with her hair intertwined with cigarette smoke. The words *"Adolph, mit Liebe auf dem 50. Geburtstag"* were written across it with the date April 20, 1939.

"To Adolph with love ..." he muttered. The woman was not Eva.

He peeked at other material his brother had put on the floor, some of it on parchment waxed and stamped with the great seal of the *Reichskanzlei.* There were also several vials in a case lined with red velvet.

"That looks like dried blood and stuff."

"Yes *trottel,* they are marked *blut, sperma.* Haven't you seen The Boys from Brazil, or even The Island of Doctor Moreau? They may not have been *au fait* with DNA in 1940 but they weren't stupid about lineage. Have you never come across the term eugenics, Moron, as in Ernst Rüdin's work on racial hygiene at St. Gallen, next door here? As in his work for the Nazi Party about unsuitables being allowed to breed ... don't you know anything?"

"Bingo again! A family tree with Uncle Adolph at the top," Ignatio said, ignoring the tirade. "What are *bingo flaps* by the way?"

An exasperated Clementino looked at his watch and decided there was no time to try bluffing an answer. The family tree was puzzling.

"And why shouldn't *der Führer* have enjoyed the fruits of the *Lebensborn* breeding programme?" he muttered, packing these finds away. "Himmler took a great interest in it. Goebbels was non-stop turning over bits on the side. Unfortunately, nobody knows how many hundreds of thousands of babies were created in this way, along with the less scientific hundreds of thousands of acceptable-looking infants kidnapped from Eastern Europe by the SS to add to the pool."

"*Bastardi ...*"

"Now, now ..."

"*... no, no ...*" Ignatio stuttered.

"I can't think of a leader who would not want to join in the fun, exercising his *droit du seigneur,* stonking every maiden in his domain. With a list like this we might even have another Billy Goat of Rey ..."

"..."

"... oh, never mind ..."

After another hour of concentrated searching they stopped what they were doing. It was after three. They were over time and had got what was required from four of the boxes. The fifth was packed with bank notes, millions-worth, Ignatio reckoned and of no interest, until he saw a ledger with the word *Portokassenbuch,* 'petty cash book,' on it. He was amused the code key, names and contact details were written on a slip of paper in the back of the book. Much more incriminating and therefore far more valuable than the dosh, or even the documents, he slipped this bonus ball into one of his zip pockets.

They got everything together they had come down with, checked with their list and began the ascent of the ladders, dragging their booty in a mail sack.

After one last chuckle from Clementino at his brother slipping into the director-general's sumptuous chair and all but disappearing beneath the elephantine desk from sheer tiredness he began untying one of their bags to stow away their packed lunches. Ignatio had a better idea. He slipped under the desk with his torch and poked around behind the central drawer.

"And what do we have here," he chortled, jangling a set of small keys on a ring, "a banker with spare keys under the plant pot. I bet he keeps PIN numbers in his wallet!"

Ignatio had planned on secreting the food where the smell of it going off could not be located, as he had done in the *direttore's* study on their last day at school.

"Hurry," said Clementino, looking at his watch as his brother fiddled with each key in turn in the central drawer, "we don't have time for this ..."

"... not even for a document beginning *Cambiale Vespucci, datata questo giorno 1 Agosto 1942!*"

"You swine, you've found the promissory note! Er, but I'm a bit short of gold bags at the moment ..."

"That's alright Brother, you can owe them to me until you cross me off the list!"

Oddly, there were several *tettarelle* in packets at the back of the drawer. Ignatio couldn't think why babies dummies should be there but now they really had to be off.

It was three forty-five and startlingly light beyond the hole in the chimney stack. They felt very exposed as they removed and bagged their second lot of onesies that were a little too colourful for comfort under the dawn sky. It was unnerving too, without the protection of a Swiss bank vault. Lights twinkled across downtown Zürich, nothing was stirring. The bricks should have been replaced loosely in the chimney to delay discovery of the manner of entry but they were definitely out of time.

Ignatio was desperate to ask his brother would they be caught "black-handed" with their loot but knew the response would not answer his question. A gusty wind was pushing them about and they wanted to crawl rather than crouch as they made their way along the red tiles below the roof crest. At least it helped muffle noise such as Ignatio's sneeze, expletives from his brother and some irreverent chuckling about Gnomes of Zürich moving assets about.

Clouds zipping by, the movement of trees below would help camouflage activity on the roof ... only a hundred metres to the skylight ... *miaow* ...

Clementino glanced at his brother.

"'Holy Mackerel' in cat burglar-speak ..."

"Oh, shut up!" he hissed, his heart thumping from the effort of having to move gear and loot in one go back to the skylight. "And keep the sack and ropes off the tiles. The last thing we want to do is a Fungus the Bogeyman and kick a tile off the roof ..."

"... that hits a police car!"

"Then we would deserve Flaked Corns for breakfast ..."

They were not out of the woods until their liaison with Wilson. And there he was, his head anyway, sticking up through the skylight, peering at his watch.

They had a quick wash, changed into their wedding finery and left the building five up from the bank shortly afterwards that Sunday morning in the same black holdalls they had arrived in. They were driven to the lay-by in the forest outside the city by Wilson and a male colleague, then the 200 kilometres to St. Moritz-Bad in a big car. The Alpha would be returned to the Bergamo car hire firm by someone else.

Because there were occasionally police about on Sunday morning all four were suited up and a little dishevelled, as if returning from a wedding reception the evening before. With all but the driver a dash of cognac served as a deodorant.

They had everything they needed in the way of wedding guest paraphernalia including a garter handed to them by My Colleague whose look defied them to comment. The booty was repacked beneath an unused bridal gown to which there was also an elaborate story attached if needed. The roads were deserted and the drive uneventful except for the views of the mountains of Central Switzerland lit by early morning sunshine.

6/3

A long shower, afternoon nap, a coded 'phone call to Papa at the villa and general kindness and feeding-up from Anna ensured there was no build-up of anti-climax after their audacity. They were now on a two-week confinement at the *palazzo*.

News can move very slowly, Wilson remarked and there might be a closing of ranks within the banking community. It was hardly likely that Nazi documents would be reported missing, so they should be prepared for disappointment. Clementino and Ignatio, the most innocent of stirrers shuddered at the forces that would be rising in apoplectic anger. They were glad to be a considerable distance from Zürich with Wilson billeted on the floor below them.

It helped that Anna took to him, the English gentleman, less, Emil's greater interest in the tall, blond muscular part. Wilson had been warned. His colleague left grinning after lunch. The boys kept to their brief of remaining inside the *contessa's* house and not showing themselves at the windows.

The next afternoon the three of them had an unsettling time poring over and cataloguing as best they could the filched material. Some of it was disappointingly mundane, some very high and mighty, even marked *Streng Geheim.* There was a good selection of the lads' signatures, Hitler, Goebbels, Himmler and gentlemen of lesser ranks but nevertheless terrible power.

Clementino was fascinated by the explanatory documents on *Hauptamt Volksdeutsche Mittelstelle,* 'Main Welfare Office for Ethnic Germans' headed paper. The reasons behind and plans for territorial expansion of a superior over inferior races, were incomprehensible.

It was a terrible thought that he and his brother being a subspecies, aristos or not, could have been experimented on or boiled down for *hors d'œuvre.* That was it, he vowed. They would be less beast to Cook and Lucciano from now on. Maybe he and his brother could initiate some 'small is beautiful' trends in an alternative television soap. Or hosting Miniature Bingo, Ignatio suggested.

Then they would make a film about a circus perhaps, with full-size people falling about in a ring and an audience entirely of Little People laughing their heads off. Hollywood should have no trouble with something silly like that.

They were very pleased to see Lucciano, two of his cousins, Umberto who was acting estate manager and Umberto's brother. These stalwarts arrived at St. Moritz-Bad in three vehicles in reassuringly sinister dark glasses, with a parcel of goodies from Cook naturally. They relieved them of the responsibility of the documents and red velvet-lined case on which was tooled in gold 'A. Hitler,' saying after the effort so far, they would guard the haul with their lives.

Over the next few days Clementino and Ignatio got into a routine of wandering down to the grotto pool before breakfast. Wilson did too but earlier. He was far too discreet to be seen anywhere other than in his room unless by invitation. The slight effervescence of the water did have a remarkable cleansing effect. Clementino felt like a sea sponge. After an hour he noticed he also looked like one.

A morning bathe set them up for breakfast. This continued with an early lunch, an early dinner, an early supper and ultimately towards the end of their third day, by boredom. Wilson obliged them on errands but they soon got bored making him run around. They didn't even have Fazio as their Whipping Boy. He was in America at Summer Camp in Yosemite. They had sent him a Good Luck post card from Italy with a suitably graphic warning about getting his head bitten off by a Grisly.

The days dragged on. It was most upsetting, the villa *excommunicado,* being audacious and ignored, champions unrecognised, heroes unsung. They tuned constantly to local radio and television and weird accents like *Züritüütsch.* Nothing. Clementino resorted to twelve hours of Country and Western from a tinny radio at his ear. Things were bad and it was fortunate the batteries expired before Ignatio exploded.

"I wonder if there's been anything reported in the Italian papers?" Ignatio asked for the umpteenth time. His brother was sitting on a large rocking horse flicking perversely through an album of family snapshots, looking for pictures of them when they were really small.

The German language newspapers perhaps, he decided. Then again it was real home-grown stuff and there had probably not been a Swiss bank robbery for fifty years, apart from the usual day-to-day dealings. Maybe there wasn't the vocabulary for such a thing in Swiss German?

What they wanted to hear was news along the lines 'bank vault barely stripped,' 'heist not, want not,' 'pile eyed on Saturday night,'

'Gnomes knocked for six.' What they got on Wednesday morning in Blick, Germany's best-known tabloid, was an item on page three beginning *"Polizeidepartement Stadt Zürich* official caught with pants down in all-night bank party."

That was the trigger. Suddenly the boys really did feel exposed. Even Wilson commented "wow!" when Emil brought in Thursday's newspapers and television and radio were turned on.

It was, however the story about the policeman, security guard, two women and a party that ran, hyped by Blick, 20 Minuten, Beobachter and the English language Swiss News. The morality of how sacrosanct is a place in which money is kept was looked at in more detail by the Zürcher Unterländer and Neue Zürcher Zeitung. An attempted robbery got a peremptory mention.

It was Herman's whereabouts in particular that captured the hacks' imagination during *Sauregurkenzeit* with a godsend of a Silly Season story. None of them or their lusty readers had any idea that the banknotes stuffed in a bra and posing pouch in the one picture of the quartet caught *in flagrante* leaked to the newspapers had come from a whip-round. This was the best laugh they'd had all year, Team One agreed, even if they had been relieved of their own cash on a bank job.

Herman maintained star billing. *"Wo ist Herman?"* and "Herman led up garden path by sister?" were questions put on the lips of those good citizens of Zürich abandoned in the town for the Summer holiday period. The story faded only after the last headline "Did Herman mastermind bungled robbery?" and was eclipsed finally by a Swiss pop singer's affair with her ex-husband and the price of cheese going up.

"All we need now," Clementino decided, "is for *Schweizer Tittle-tattler* to feature us on its front page in an exclusive interview from a secret third floor location in St. Moritz-Bad, next door to the Hotel ..."

"Just think, us and million-franc bingo ads on the front page!"

"And a mass gathering of baying Neo-Nazis on the edge of town."

If the first half of the week was slow in confinement, the second did not move at all. It was a tragedy because just outside the front door was sunshine, coffee and pastries, pecan ice-cream, cold beer and girl-watching going to waste. Worse was the tantalization of the August holiday funfair and nearby circus. The high point of St. Moritz festivities that year, the *Dampfmaschine Rallye,* 'Steam Traction Engine Rally,' was something they were really miserable at missing out on.

They had to be content with perusing the huge valley panorama with field glasses and their own cold beer and *bretzeln* in the *palazzo's* empty attic rooms. They could see lines of red, green and black engines, frilly canopies, black smoke belching from little chimneys and the occasional puff of steam. On that Friday night, the fifth night of torture, the tremolo of a carousel organ, adult female squealing and the brasher sounds of a musical genre common to fairgrounds the world over would take them up to eleven. A myriad of mirrors and coloured light bulbs completed a magical scene, all just a kilometre away.

Ignatio sighed.

"I have this almost overwhelming urge to pop out for a hot dog. But we couldn't possibly disobey orders ..."

"Of course not," Clementino replied clicking his heels from a seated position, this time from behind an Italian newspaper. "It would be unthinkable."

Ignatio perfected the angle of his greased-down fringe emulating the beginning of a comb-over and touched up his moustache with some of Kunz's eye-liner and silver glitter he found in Fazio's room. Several souvenir snaps of the *Führer* were laid out for reference. He was also wearing his top hat and crumpled wedding suit marvelling at how a little make-up had transformed him from mere 'Leader' to 'Great Dictator.'

"I wonder if the *bancarella di hamburger* is up by the *birreria* tent this year?"

"Our Man with the Mango Sauce!"

"Do you remember the time we sampled everything?"

"Popcorn, bevanda frizzante, hot dogs, zucchero filato, gelato Americano ..."

Clementino could have added more, drink especially but did not want to be sick again. The only thing stopping them venturing out that night was a British rock band making a howling noise that wolves would have steered clear of across the mountains.

Penny Lane goes to Italy

7/1

The normal routine quickly returned to the Saltzmann Schweinchencommerzbank after the holiday weekend, though town would remain quiet through August. The more nervous customers were reassured their money was safe. Some commercial accounts were less than complimentary about security. Others tutted vigorously about the rubbish the popular press was churning out. One elderly woman from the South-east said when Romansh was spoken everywhere there wasn't that kind of disrespect. Saltzmann's staff dealt with it all.

The only sign of anything extraordinary having happened was the appearance of two daytime security guards, one of whom paced up and down the street in a neatly-pressed uniform trying not to looked bored witless. There were also two no-nonsense night-time tough guys, neither of whom was Herman.

Saltzmann failed miserably in his attempt at avoiding publicity. Journalists, a lone *paparazzo*, radio presenters and television crews pestered him and his staff day and night for a week. A Channel Four Radio News van became a permanent feature of a nearby restricted parking area and got several tickets. Television people caught him outside the tradesman's entrance at dawn and at the front door of his house at midnight.

It is an "impenetrable vault," they fled "empty-handed," their antics were "laughable," *Generaldirektor* Saltzmann bleated.

SRF 1's *Schweiz Aktuell* team were the first to comment on his appearance on their evening slot trapping him again coming out of nearby Saint Peter's Church in darkness. He looked haggard, his eyes bulged but he got no mercy from their anchorman who was as brassy as she was on screen, only smaller.

It was a particularly pushy journalist from SRF 1's *Zürich Schaffhausen* who managed to get a more personal interview in a darkened street near Saltzmann's home in plush residential Dolder on the Adlisberg mountain north-east of the city.

How often did parties like this occur at the bank ... did he ever join them ... didn't he feel sorry for the embarrassment it must have caused Herman's mother ... can't a man have a bit of fun on his birthday? He was not impressed with the banker's mumblings. It didn't give him much to work on but the chase made a change from sniffing around Tyco International or the Riesling industry for a usually, insipid story. Saltzmann kept his mouth shut about Herman having been fired and in a very delicate state in a nearby psychiatric unit.

From the moment of the senior clerk's telephone call to Saltzmann's home advising him of the robbery, Saltzmann began twitching. A break-in with or without money being taken he could cope with. A single ripe raspberry on greaseproof paper on his desk he could not. He summoned the cleaning supervisor. She left it where she found it, she said, early that morning. Saltzmann asked if she had noticed anything else unusual about the office. Perfectly tidy, she said. She had wiped and straightened his chair and the fireplace back plate. There was a lot of soot on the carpet which had taken a while to vacuum. She assumed it was blown down the chimney by the wind over the weekend.

Saltzmann began sweating. The break-in had centred around the basement and security office below him. His office had remained locked. He left the bank at five that afternoon but was back an hour later after the last of his staff had gone, his gaunt appearance unnerving the new security men. Ignoring the fact his wife had telephoned several times, he locked himself in his office and sat almost motionless at his desk. This was the first time that busy day he could access the vault boxes and he wished he did not know what was coming.

First, he opened his right-hand desk drawer and fingered the toy Luger. How he wanted it to be real. Then he rummaged for a new dummy, saw the Italian promissory note had gone and began shaking. When he reached the vault at the bottom of the ladders and saw sacred papers, Party history, the *Stalhelm's* heritage strewn along the narrow concrete passageway he felt pain in his chest. All five of their boxes had been rifled and he saw immediately documents and items were missing. Petty cash looked intact but his palpitations returned on realising the cash book had been taken. He had to sit down. When he thought it couldn't get any worse he saw marks on all the other flaps.

As the week wore on, the *Generaldirektor's* behaviour grew odder. He asked his assistant about flights to Asunción and other destinations in South America, then Moscow, then, sod it, Phuket. He rang his insurance company to ask about extending his life cover then hung up knowing he would get nowhere with that except deeper into suspicion. He was told repeatedly by the switchboard in the college at Würzburg the extension he was asking for did not exist.

At lunchtime on Thursday amidst the continuing mayhem of press, police and other officials there was a sighting of him in a boat on the lake. He appeared to have a bucketful of jellybeans he was scattering across the water.

By Friday, with Herman stories at least taking the heat off the fact that robbers had succeeded in accessing and damaging the main vault door, Saltzmann's favoured option in an otherwise state of complete torpor remained suicide. Lack of sleep caused by haunting visions of empty boxes was affecting his concentration on the slightest of tasks.

A discreet enquiry came through from Würzburg eventually and he returned a message of reassurance. It did not reassure. Early the following Saturday morning *Herr* Vogler was waiting in his office. Otto Vogler was nearby in Bavaria when he was instructed to leave a 'calling card' with *Herr* Saltzmann. This man, in his eighties like Rothenfelder was the founder of a sports equipment manufacturing company in Frankfurt and a physical fitness fanatic. He was responsible for the world-wide recruiting of agents to serve the cause. His department was the most secret within the *Stalhelm*, its cell structure and how it was co-ordinated being known only to him.

Vogler was also of Hitler Youth and an official in the *KdF*, *Kraft durch Freude*, 'Strength through Joy,' the organization that controlled German workers after the trade unions were neutralized in the 1930s. His motto *Gleichschaltung*, 'coordination,' was as potent a euphemism in Nazi Germany as 'final solution' and use of the word today is avoided because of the connotation.

"You fool, Saltzmann, *idiot, blödel, vollkoffer* ..." he raged from the moment the director-general walked in to his own office, "... a trunk, Ming vases, a hole in the chimney, a raspberry, MIDGETS in our bank ... why does the organization carry such imbeciles ... yes, it can only be the Vespuccis ... who did you think it was, *Weihnachtsmann und seine Elfen ... Schneewittchen bei ihrem eigenen ...*"

The hole had only just been discovered by the builders surveying the damage. Saltzmann explained it away as a lightning strike. By their head-shaking about Acts of God it seemed they believed him. It didn't stop Vogler shouting for what seemed an hour. The organization's worry he ranted, was not piddling little things like the theft of a National Socialist archive of which they were guardians in perpetuity, a comprehensive list of cash contributors and high blood pressure at his age. It was about the dangers of a FINMA enquiry, one that could blow the whole organization open and compromise the integrity of the entire Neo-Nazi movement around the world.

Still quivering with rage, the German walked slowly around Saltzmann who had all but disappeared into his chair. He spotted the Luger in a partly-open drawer, took it out, pointed it at Saltzmann's head and pulled the trigger. A flag with *paff!* written on it popped out of the barrel and amused him.

Confirmation of the robbery came in a registered package the following Monday morning. It was a letter signed by Herman Goering in his capacity as *Reichsstatthalter* and it brought Saltzmann to his knees. It was confirmation his end was near. And how he wished he was going out in a blaze of glory, even though the commendation was for Oflag IV-C *Kommandant* Oberst Schmidt preventing escape from Colditz Castle. That was before April 1941, after which escape became routine.

With this magnificent, yellowing document was a page torn from the back of an Italian diary on which was written in German,

"Eight hundred million Swiss Francs please, for eighty-six items 'of interest.' A mixture of currencies and bonds (not more than 50% of the total amount) is acceptable. We require *volle Zahlung (pagamento totale)* and considering your recent level of service, we will be changing our bank."

Beneath it, as if it needed signing, was drawn another raspberry.

"Enough ..." Rothenfelder snapped at the *Stalhelm* meeting convened in Würzburg a few days later. It was extraordinary enough for the dispensing with the need to interlock six pieces of a steel helmet on its wooden head. "I have heard enough of how our banker has been reduced to a snivelling wreck. A calling card was left and we need his professional front until this business is concluded. So, *Herren*, we come to *Einsatz Wecht*. Or perhaps it will make the point more in their own tongue, *Operazione Nani."*

No one was in the mood to smile about yet another reference to midgets or dwarves. Kleper and several of his colleagues were already in the vicinity of the Vespucci villa north of Bergamo. Vogler and his team were on their way to St. Moritz. A Vespucci cousin, the *Marquise Anna Raffino von Bergamo* lived there and the family probably considered it an ideal place at which robbers could hide their loot, or even hide. They were dealing with amateurs, good amateurs but Italian nevertheless.

The fact that an *Engländer* and *Geheimwaffe,* 'secret weapon' were involved, Rothenfelder heard, caused him to tap his fingers. This was a very bad sign and most of them around the table cringed. Fortunately their leader chose not to go off on that tangent for the moment. He calmly reminded everyone no stone should be left unturned. If the two *kleiner Mensch* moved a centimetre, they would have them. They did not need little red costumes and white beards to be picked out in a crowd. He suggested they could lose one. The second they should be more careful with.

Rothenfelder closed the meeting by thanking Schumacher and his team for the speed with which they put together *Operazione Nani*. They would meet again the following Saturday morning to discuss the outcome. It would not fail with the expertise and resources allocated to it.

7/2

"Oh, how sweet Mummy, there's a clown!"

The child spoke in English but Ignatio knew what she was referring to and wondered if he still had his *Führer* face on. She was actually pointing to Clementino nearby climbing a ladder against a wheel twice his height on probably the biggest steam engine at the fair. Ignatio warmed to the idea and was annoyed he hadn't thought of it, a clown disguise. He and his brother knew all about pushing each other around. There was an International Circus on the lake shore and they must have been about. Then he decided a pair of clowns would be the first thing hoodlums would look for if someone had just turned over their bank.

He rested where he was beneath the counter of a stall selling old chocolates, according to the date on the cartons. He was keeping a look out but was finding it hard picking out legs that might belong to thugs from the endless pairs passing him. They would hardly be wearing *Wehrmacht* green, or worse, black SS trousers and leather jackboots.

His brother's legs and little boots he saw flash by. There was a yelp from a large disgruntled dog. Ignatio realised his brother had been spotted when a pair of ominous-looking trousers stopped suddenly by the chocolates turning one way, then the other. He held his breath as polished toe caps poked under the chocolate stall's white and red rayon covers to within an inch of his nose.

The man was fumbling with an ammunition clip, using the Swiss national colours for cover. The pistol he was sporting was however, Austrian. Knowing about these things Ignatio was surprised it was a Steyr, a lady's pistol. In fact it was such a puny weapon he thought of tying the shoelaces together for a laugh, until shooting started nearby.

You wouldn't think fairground whooping and screaming could get any more panicky, unless Godzilla was on the horizon. It did. Then the shooting stopped suddenly and there was an eerie silence. Ignatio peaked from his cover. His brother was nowhere to be seen and for a moment he felt curiously detached in thinking he might have copped it from a lady's pistol. The notion of 'served him right' flashed through his mind, unable to turn down an invitation into the cab of one of the Puffing Billys. It was the biggest in the show, a John Fowler & Co. Supreme Showman's Engine of 1930 vintage, according to the sign. Irresistible to a little show-off.

What to do next was decided by the return of the trousers and pistol. Recklessly, Ignatio grabbed at the gun. It went off in the direction of the owner's polished shoes. There was a shriek but not from Ignatio even though he was sprawled over boxes of a beaming Dr. Sprungli's Mountain Rose selection. He was chuckling from the pop of the puny weapon and it having stopped its owner in his tracks. Nevertheless, he thought it prudent to back away through some canvas screening onto sawdust. Realisation of where he was came with a wooden ball about to hit his head.

The man who threw the ball gaped at the little figure laid out cold amongst the Aunt Sallies. Those next to him, apparently oblivious to gunshots and screaming from the aisle at the other end of the shy, chose to see a funny side. Wilson was not one of them.

Tipped off by Kunz about the silence from the floor above him at the *palazzo*, the Englishman loaded his sidearm and headed for the fairground. He caught sight of Ignatio in the little plantation of coconuts on poles. He didn't have time to warn Ignatio to duck, or run. He vaulted the counter, picked up Ignatio's limp body and ran the length of the shy with him under his arm, like a body-snatcher.

Bullets kicked up dirt and snapped through canvas. One whistled by his head and passed through a coconut that remained suspiciously on its stand. He found a way through to the adjacent hoop-la stall where another bullet took out a doll on the shelf above him. The stall holder looked surprised and bent down to pick it up. It was lucky he did for bullets splattered three more of the delicate pig-tailed dolls causing them to fall grinning to the grass and him to spread-eagle next to them quivering.

Wilson next found himself halfway up a rifle range and moved swiftly for the cover of the boards at the head of this classic fairground entertainment. Ignatio was still under his arm. He dragged the startled owner to the ground just as a volley of shots passed over them finding several of the range's targets. Two ducks were sent winging to the roof. A battleship was blasted off its mounts. Bells dinged alarmingly.

Confusion set in as people realised something serious was happening in the failing light. Women screamed. Several men dived for cover, one pulling a child with him whose head disappeared into a ball of pink *zucchero filato*. Others scattered as four of the thugs advanced on the rifle range blatantly now, Lugers blasting.

Wilson slapped Ignatio a couple of times telling him to collect his wits. He searched for a gap in the wooden boarding they were crouched behind, poked one of the Winchesters through and fired three shots in quick succession. He hit his nearest foe in the leg. The other two Germans looked at each other in surprise, then at the range, then took cover, pulling their whining colleague with them.

The stall holder reached for more rifles and ammunition with a look of glazed euphoria on his face rendered ghastly by yellow and orange bulbs and a red glow from the sky.

"For twenty years," he began in the Romansh tongue which neither Wilson nor a groggy Ignatio understood a word of, "I have watched idiots make silly comments and miss these dumb targets. And now whoever you are, whoever they are, I'm going to do what I've barely been able to resist all these years ..."

"Nazi ..." mumbled a groggy Ignatio watching the man take aim at something.

"Ne! Rätoromanisch ..." came the indignant response.

Bullets whanged, fine china exploded and goldfish bowls shattered, cascading water and fish over cuddly toys. Light bulbs popped, people screamed, the music played on. A popcorn machine began smoking, a bullet having passed through its motor. An orange juice dispenser sprouted one, then three leaks as three Winchesters got a simultaneous fix on one of the bully-boys cowering behind it. It was an elderly woman who got juiced up, the thugs having backed away dragging their injured colleague with them.

Vogler and his team were now twenty minutes into *Operazione Nani* and losing the battle. Both Vespucci *Zwerge* were cornered but they had not reckoned on resistance from the rifle range and a steam engine preventing them from being snatched. They had only a few minutes before the police got through the throngs higher up the hill. It was time to disappear. More specifically, it was time for Vogler to disappear.

Some in the crowd indicated frantically to Wilson the direction in which the gunmen were retreating. Others were not so friendly with their gestures. Wilson beckoned Ignatio to follow him, saying they had to find Clementino. He thanked the stallholder for the use of the rifles while indicating a curve like a banana's. Euphoria disappeared from the man's face as he remonstrated in broken English,

"But I have to make a living ..."

Clementino was unharmed having ducked into a whirly-gig control booth when shooting started. He was concerned it related to Ignatio and hoped the lure of chocolate sampling would keep him under the stall. He then collided with a huge St. Bernard called Kitty slobbering over what looked like a dozen hot dogs on a paper plate with mustard, ketchup and onions and wasn't surprised at overhearing its owner say "one hundred kilos ..." to a fascinated onlooker. He returned to the presumed safety of a great green, black, red and silver boiler-plated beast now glowing, dripping water and wrinkling the sky with heat from its smoke stack.

The engine's keeper, a grimy-faced individual with a black beret, spotted red kerchief and Lancashire accent that Ignatio barely recognised as English, was adding smoke handsomely from a meerschaum pipe the colour of sunset over the Ruhr. He had warmed to Clementino popping his head over the rail to introduce himself

and say he was in a spot of bother. When gunfire started he decided to get some steam up.

Only moments later the crowd by his engine scattered, two bullets zinged off the front wheels and a third off the underside of the no-nonsense canopy blowing all his light bulbs in one go. He hauled Clementino onto the man stand, pushed the ladder away, used his shovel to rap the knuckles of someone trying to climb up the back and resumed stoking the fire box awkwardly on one knee. The on-lookers were now just three leering gunmen re-loading their pistols. In a few seconds the Little Vespucci would be theirs.

Clementino chose then to make polite conversation about the engine. It went something like,

"How did you get it here from Lancashire …"

"By road …"

"How long did that take …"

Another gunman clambered aboard a more modest engine on their left and Clementino was grateful his new buddy was preparing the Fowler for motion. The answer to his last question he was sure was "twelve month." He amused himself in his mother tongue with a comment of "plenty of time for sightseeing" before marvelling at the consummate ease with which the mighty engine crept forward, hissing and belching, cams, rods and levers back and forth and enough black smoke from the stack to screen a battleship.

"Madre Mia..." he began in wonderment, ducking again as a bullet whizzed past.

Still puffing steadily on the pipe between clenched teeth the driver alternated a vigorous turning of the larger of two chromium wheels with adjusting levers. Only when they reached walking pace did he lean out to get a bearing.

"Is tha fussed about direction ..."

Catching his drift, Clementino pulled himself up one of the barley-twist canopy supports to see what was ahead and was only just saved by a burly arm from the flywheel. People scattered as they puffed their way down the main promenade past a long line of engines. The shooting stopped and they began the descent of a nerve-wrackingly dark alpine pasture to the fairground's car park and exit.

Here was line upon line of pristine vehicles against a backdrop of snow-capped peaks of the Upper Engadin. Peeking again, Clementino noticed three Mercedes-Benz cars sporting brazen 'SS' number plates parked separately. A wild excitement took hold. Two of the shooters were running towards the cars. Two others leaning on each other stopped, stricken with terror at a beast from Revelation bearing down on them blowing steam from its belly and smoke and glowing cinders into the night sky. The blue flashing lights of police Volkswagens in the distance added urgency.

"The Mercs, the Mercs ... kill, kill ..." Clementino shouted in a frenzy of lust.

"Toss coal in t' box, lad ... careful now ..." the driver muttered coolly. "The wife stokes but she went f'a beer."

A few more metres and there was screaming, male for a change. Clementino cheered manically as the Supreme pushed the first silver-white car against the second and rose above both shuddering. There was a groaning and rending of metal, popping of fine leather upholstery, boom of exploding tyres and more delicate sound of grinding glass and crunching of a CD player. The music didn't stop. That was coming from somewhere else. The cars passed gently beneath an unforgiving back wheel

His heart was in his mouth as they levelled out. The driver turning the wheel vigorously, both hands on its little wooden knob, his biceps bulging, concerned they could topple over on the slope. Clementino reached for the chain he was sure would release a triumphal blast only to cackle uncontrollably at the delicate 'peep, peep.'

The wide-eyed driver of the third Mercedes now rammed full like a Keystone Cops vehicle was struggling with automatic shift, its rear wheels skidding on the grass. He banged it into reverse, rammed someone's treasured little four-by-four, panicked at the thirty-ton monster looming in the darkness and kicked the driver's door open. The other three doors were opened likewise. There was more screaming and the 'cops' piled out as though they had been rehearsing the manoeuvre for a month.

That was how that car met its fate, reduced to half a metre in height in the springy Alpine turf, like a butterfly on a pin. Its four doors were flattened and window glass in thousands of cubes was scattering the fairground's myriad of coloured bulbs and last of the evening light dropping behind the mountains.

Otto Vogler walked casually back up the hill into town, a good citizen enjoying the fun of the fair, as they had when they were young, when everyone was young and the world was full of hope. There were police everywhere now. They had begun marshalling the exiting crowds. He pushed past two elderly ladies and dropped his pistol, wiped clean, into one of the lady's straw baskets. He raised his hat politely apologising for his haste. He raised his hat again to a young policeman and walked on.

He was too old for this sort of thing he muttered to himself. They were all getting too old. Someone would pay for the brawling senior Party members had been reduced to that evening. Saltzman would get a thrashing he would never forget. It was time also for some retirement, beginning with Rothenfelder's.

Penny Lane goes to Italy

8/1

The Italo-English camp got the message about the lengths the Neo-Nazi organization behind the bank would go to in retrieving its property and/ or in not paying its bills. Two weeks after the robbery, Clementino and Ignatio were brought back to the villa at Bergamo. Their father, Lucciano, his cousin and two other relatives and Wilson with backup formed a convey of five vehicles that travelled at speed, lights blazing, sometimes with horns blaring.

"Two can play this game," went through Vespucci's mind as he cut corners and other cars up in a country where driving is of a generally high standard but where drivers take liberties. It is hardly surprising, he thought, with poor street lighting, inadequate safety at road works and with road marking and signing almost non-existent. At least they were far enough north not to have cars with Cuneo plates getting in their way.

His aggression was not because of other drivers. His son was in the back with a bullet wound in his shoulder, fortunately comfortable and not in danger. He was seriously considering ordering a more powerful Range Rover with bullet-proof glass and armour plating. The hornets' nest they had stirred would not settle in a hurry.

The boys were happy lying low on back seats under cover for the four-hour drive, one with Papa and the other with Wilson. They were in good spirits. Ignatio was singing lustily in English, *"I owe, I owe, it's off to work I go ..."* still amused at seeing this on a plate on the back of a car in London. He was practising his English in making up a suitable rest of verse. His father was barely listening.

Clementino travelling with Wilson managed eight verses of *"There were eggs, eggs, that walked on little legs in the stores ... in the stores ..."* The Brits were highly amused he should know such an idiosyncratic British ditty, many of whose verses they had not heard. He learnt them from an English pen friend dragged around the world by her parents in Her Majesty's Armed Forces.

It was dark when the convoy arrived at the villa after a nervy last twenty minutes through the *Parco* north of Branzi. There were many twists and turns where they could have been ambushed and it was a relief to see Umberto at the gate with several armed estate workers. He had mustered twenty, all good men.

Most were posted around the villa. There were boxes of cartridges everywhere, some hard liquor and a grim silence from the shadows. Vespucci thought he even saw the flash of teeth, like those of Mexican *desperados* on American actor salaries. All of them were steeped in the stories their fathers had told often about the SS retreating up the valley. They would be standing no nonsense on this occasion.

The local doctor was on hand to dress Ignatio's flesh wound. He gave him painkillers and an injection of antibiotics and stressed the shoulder needed resting. During the excitement of the first round of shooting at the coconut shy Ignatio did not notice he was wounded. Only after an hour and some nagging pain and seeing dried blood on his hand did he realise.

Ironically, confinement at the villa was a more miserable affair. There was nothing beyond their windows but the tranquillity of vineyards, orchards and majestic mountains. It was difficult enough keeping away from the windows during the day. Towards dusk, every shutter around the house was closed creating a deathly silence. They were in a mausoleum. Every little noise retained in the old house offered no comfort, water pipes knocking, toilets flushed, occasional footsteps along marble corridors, dormice in the walls, moaning in the chimneys, 'Rico, raucous from lack of attention and the racket Clementino was making in the north wing with his music.

Wilson and his colleague departed, their role in the operation having ended. They would miss the razzmatazz, colourful characters and Vespucci hospitality, they said. Wilson couldn't even leave his telephone number. There was no chance he could pop back from his next gig in Papua New Guinea. He was not actually there, he added discretely. He just wanted to affirm he really was not available.

Vespucci was obliged to venture out to the Milan textiles mills and canning plant in Naples after the weekend. He took with him an armed escort of two of his relatives to the huge suspicion of the management and work force at both sites. He worked late into the evening for the rest of the week seemingly unperturbed by the possibility, even probability of a gang of Nazi thugs skulking outside the villa's gates. They would be sitting it out he told his sons until Saltzmann, their only contact with the presumed Neo-Nazi organization behind the bank, responded to the family's polite request for its money.

He did think about his son's concerns of *Panzer* driving through the gates, as it had done in the recent past. As traumatic, he replied emphasizing the improbability, was his son's attempt at demolishing the gates some time later with his little yellow roadster.

That third week of August was unusually hot and airless because of the closed shutters and limited air-conditioning missing a regular thump from Lucciano. He was outside much of the time during the night jollying the men along, passing around cigarettes and snacks.

Vespucci was backwards and forwards between library and study. Not because he was constantly referring to the sumptuous and valuable collection of books but to top up his drink. During the last renovation of his working area he had a bar built into the library behind bookcases that parted electronically.

He was particularly pleased with the way concealed up-lighters beneath shelves of old cognacs and ports added appropriate alcoholic hues to the Giordano ceiling with its already red-faced cherubs and nymphs. Directly above the bar was a group holding bunches of grapes paying homage to a curvy Dionysus. He regretted not having the courage to ask the artist who did the restoration to re-model this figure on a picture of his wife at eighteen years of age when they had just married.

Clementino didn't leave his apartment for the first week. He spent one afternoon tinkering with the pensive G minor Adagio by Albinoni that everyone thinks is the only piece he wrote. It was true he didn't write much. He didn't even write this piece. It was composed in 1958 by Remo Giazotto.

Never mind neo-Baroque, Clementino thought, his version would be the one remembered. He had speeded it up, fiddled about with it in his tape-editing machine and turned it into a bouncy little number with plenty of syncopation. He then played it endlessly through the evening at enormous volume, grinding his teeth at the masochism. By ten o'clock he was bored with that and reverted to flicking through copies of Playmen.

Three weeks after the robbery, Ignatio too was beyond being restless. If he didn't get out that night it would be the third Saturday he had not seen Gabrielle at 1783. She would be very worried if they missed their *appuntamento* again knowing he and his brother had gone to Zürich on a mission to collect some important papers belonging to the family, as he had put it. He wanted desperately to report with a big smile the family business was safe for another day. He wouldn't tell her it had entailed dropping into a bank after hours. Explaining a bullet wound would also be tricky.

Contrary to his father's strictest instructions not to leave his room and the first time in a long time he had disobeyed him, that year anyway, he got himself ready to go out. What Vespucci had not got across to his sons was the danger just beyond the gate. What Ignatio couldn't do until he was face to face with Gabrielle was warn her to stay away from the estate until matters had been resolved. She was in danger also.

Lucciano was patrolling the corridors inside the house as well as moving around outside on his vigil. His cousin Mauro, not missing an opportunity to make himself bodily comfortable had opted for the coolest place on the estate, sharing space with the clock in the little tower on the main outbuilding. He was on watch from midnight and had got into the habit of taking with him a bottle of wine and some salami or ham and a little mustard from the kitchen. Ignatio needed to be most careful of him, if he hadn't dozed off. The tower commanded the best view of the boundary of the house and its gardens with the orchard and vineyards.

Then Ignatio had an idea. He would climb over the roof to his brother's side of the villa and go down that way. If he was seen, Clementino would get bawled out. He was apprehensive with his arm in a sling because the roof, even with discreet and permanent roping, was tricky at the best of times. At eleven-thirty, when Lucciano had passed his door, he pulled himself with some discomfort onto the roof over his bedroom. At his bathroom skylight he wished he had remembered to turn his lights off. If anyone had been looking, even from a kilometre away he would have been very visible.

Pressing on through the shadows created by the villa's huge ornate chimneys he edged his way along a cornice and gable before crawling between glazed sections over his brother's apartment. The glow in the bedroom was from the aquarium in the wall. He had fixed a large convex lense to the front of it that hugely magnified the school of Piranhas. Many an unsuspecting female friend had screamed at the teeth looming unexpectedly at great speed with an audible snap from behind the glass.

"What in Heaven's name ..." he muttered. Just below him in the centre of the studio was a huge spot-lit canvas, a portrait of *la Beata Vergine*. It was not the usual long-faced Mary in unsullied white wimple and unruffled Cerulean Blue robe dreamt up to make all dumpy Italian women feel inadequate. He had captured the pose perfectly, fettered by beads and crucifix, head bent under the weight of her halo and two *millennia* of moral responsibility. It was Fat-face Sophie. A female arm in the picture with its hand up this Virgin's dress was the confirmation.

"He's finally flipped," Ignatio muttered, "and turned to religion. Or sex and religion. Either way, he's not getting it ..."

Since he and his brother were very small they had come and gone to their rooms as they pleased up the side of a building with many decorative features in the brickwork. Footholds they referred to them as. Extra help was provided by pitons. Papa still did not know it was pitons, not screw bolts securing the drainpipe brackets to the wall on two sides of the villa. They could do it blindfold, though not, Ignatio realised, with one arm tied behind your back.

As he edged along the parapet some twenty metres off the ground he knew he would have to undo his sling and use one of the many ropes neatly coiled behind the ledge. To be safe, he selected the one marked '3 m' that meant it was three metres short of the ground and could not be seen at night. It was a bit of a drop to the paving but he would risk not rolling on his dodgy shoulder. To get back up to his apartment he only needed to pull some well-hidden string for an *étrier* to come tumbling down. Climbing one of these was equally arduous, even with two good arms but it wasn't going to stop him that night.

It was a joy being out of a stuffy house. He heard talking and saw the glow of a cigarette on the other side of the garden. He moved stealthily through the *parterre,* crawled across the lawn, slipped past the two men by the tractor shed door and raced up the rutted track to the orchard and 1783. It was a little after midnight, the appointed place and time but there was no sign of life. There was no message in the wall, only silence beneath a million stars.

Sitting on a stone shivering a little without a jacket he wondered if Lella might be at the château or at her little library above the garage. Maybe she had left a message there on her way to the archway or perhaps on her way back home.

Since their first meeting when she had slipped on the ice he had been uncomfortable with how much he owned, enjoyed and even threw away compared with her few possessions. His interpretation of this was that she actually had nothing. She was perfectly happy, she said, with her brothers and sisters and father and a few treasured photographs of her mother. He tried giving her things. He wanted to give her everything but she dismissed the very notion. It meant nothing at all to her.

Then, one evening she let slip she liked books. There had never been books in the house, her schooling was cut short and she really wanted to read, to learn, she said. It was the chink in the armour. When he said the Chinese have a proverb that a book is like a garden in your pocket she was so impressed. She was sure she could become wise and knowledgeable if she had books all around her.

It was while they were sitting giggling in the Estate Manager's 1911 motor car in a corner of the outbuilding one night he had a brilliant idea. They had pulled its covering back and she was at the wheel. They were amused because neither of them had hands strong enough to sound the bulb horn. Gabrielle had never  seen such an old car, or one as grand. This French company, Panhard-Levasseur was favoured by Russian aristocracy Ignatio said. Perhaps, he suggested, it could have been driven by the Tsar himself in the days before the Revolution.

That settled it. He couldn't imagine being without his books. He would build her a private library. There were two large closets on the floor above the car, one of which had a separate toilet and basin. The closet was big enough to sit and read in. It had a window with shutters and a substantial door. Lucciano confirmed nobody ever went into this outbuilding.

Over the next few weeks Ignatio cleaned and decorated the little room and fitted shelving and a new lock. He rewired the light and switch, putting in something more friendly for reading. He cobbled together a hoist and winch to get a small table and discarded but rather nice padded leather chair up the staircase.

He even cleaned the toilet after asking a very curious maid how best to do this. She gave him a bottle of strong acid, the type sold in all supermarkets next to the 95% industrial alcohol always on the bottom shelves, as if children would not be drawn to skulls and crossbones. Big mistake, of course, as that same day everyone wanted to know why the Younger wanted to know how to clean toilets. It was a big story for a short time.

At least he was sure after his renovation work he and Gabrielle held the only keys. She had her own key to the back door as well and her own gate through which she could come and go from the vineyard. He did agonise over wanting to convert the rest of the mezzanine into a refuge. The second closet would have been a perfect kitchen and the rest of the floor a wonderful open-plan bed-sitting room.

Stocking the library was the easy part, even though Gabrielle was not forthcoming about what she wanted to read. She only said, with heart-breaking sadness she would be grateful for anything he put there.

Two months after its conception, everything he could lay his hands on went in, from Mao's Little Red Book from his *fascista* brother's bookshelves, to a sumptuous turn-of-the-century copy of the Catholic Church's *Index Librorum Prohibitorum* he hoped Papa would not ask after. There were Asterix albums in three languages he and Clementino had learnt their Gallo-Roman history from, children's books they had learnt some of their English and German from and other useful things like the Haynes Manuals for cars he had owned.

He sneaked into the kitchen to see what Cook was reading and was very surprised. While there he lifted the less spattered of two copies of *Marcella Cucina* and other cookery books, leaving one by someone called Delia Smith that looked a bit cobbled together. He also included one of his own *Larousse Gastronomique* editions. It was in French but if ever there was an incentive for someone interested in food to learn the language, this was it.

Literature ranged from Hardy and Tolstoy to Collette and Balzac. Odd volumes he grabbed included Kant's Critique and several Barbara Cartland stories. He remembered these being described as *corset rip-offs,* with millions of English and American women learning about life and love through reading them. Always big swarthy blokes and frilly waifs on the covers, naturally. He was pleased with the shelf of illustrated books on art, music and architecture. Biography was lacking and he would rectify this next time he was in Bergamo.

It was only when the room was about stuffed to capacity he admitted to himself he actually had no idea what seventeen year-old girls read in lighter moments. Off he went to his favourite bookshop, Libreria. *Chick Lit* he was assured was the thing and he emerged with a bagful.

While he was in town he bought current issues of the glossies Amica and Grazia and decided he would keep these and other fashion magazines a regular feature of the library. Perhaps one day he would see a woman he knew actually wearing one of these creations, actually smiling and not plodding pouting down a catwalk. He could but dream.

He thought long and hard about the artistic and literary merits of Playmen and the American version Playboy, then decided he didn't want to get slapped. Likewise with Marquis de Sade *erotica,* which he found difficult to read anyway. Anaïs Ninn was more sensual and he thought he would try his blooming young woman with Delta of Venus and Little Birds and hold his breath.

Absolutely essential were the classic poems and love stories. Flicking through some of the books he wondered why he should not write a *Romeo e Gabrielle.* Their relationship was like an unfolding tragedy of disparate families and forbidden love. And why shouldn't he write a sonnet a day for a year as Petrarcha had done for his 'Lella' in *Canzoniere?* He consoled himself with the thought that everything already out there was new to the girl, the 154 *Sonetti di Shakespeare*, Boccaccio's *Decamarone* and Chaucer's *I Racconti di Canterbury.*

And so it went on, Dante, Machiavelli, Nostradamus, the *Costituzione della Repubblica italiana* ... The range was infinite. Sadly, space wasn't.

His greater angst was them never being together long enough to discuss the books. He was gratified nevertheless, she was soon reading avidly. When he occasionally wandered up to the outbuilding late at night to squeeze more in he saw the neat piles on the table and titles on the shelves had been rearranged. There were tell-tale gaps. He made sure there were torches and batteries, worried always about her out alone on the mountainside, sometimes in total darkness, even though she said she was used to it. He was desperate to bump into her there but understood this was her private time and space and he must respect it.

Desperate also to give his girlfriend more personal things, he was delighted she accepted *cioccolatini* now and again. She was embarrassed with the huge box he gave her on their first *Giorno di San Valentino.* She admitted months later she put a few of the chocolates into a paper bag and had to throw the rest away because her siblings, her father, would have asked questions.

Signora at the tiny shop in Via Sant'Alessandro was very helpful. Like perfume and flowers, the *chocolatier* said, watching him choosing pieces he obviously liked, a gift of chocolates can range between inappropriate and overpowering. She asked the age of his *ragazza* and made a selection on his behalf. The little note Lella left after that first box read simply "thank you so much for the chocolates. I ate one and floated over the mountain! A big hug for my man xx." He left the choosing to the *Signora* after this.

It was much later he learned she shared them with her siblings. He had wondered why she liked them in sixes or twelves. It made them much better value, she wrote, multiplying the enjoyment by six!

Strangely, now feeling responsible for someone, perhaps several people for the first time in his life he had a moment of sadness at not having a mother, or rather, never knowing her. He remembered a line in Tolstoy "a man learns most in the company of clever women." Having a mother was surely a good start?

He had been shocked one evening driving the long way around on the SP1 and SP2 into the mountains to Fóppolo then up the steep track through the pine forest past their run-down farm. Gabrielle's father concentrated on timber cutting and milling. Her three younger brothers and two sisters took care of a small area of maize and an extensive vegetable-growing area that included potatoes, lettuce and soft fruits. Gabrielle and Paolo were responsible for the sheep that grazed the steep meadows above and below the house.

When Ignatio told her what he had done she begged him never to do it again. He was very unhappy he said, about her difficulties with her father and reasoned that should she ever need to escape she would have a little bedsit, a little home of her own. She looked horrified again and told him firstly she had a responsibility to her brothers and sisters. Secondly the farm was her home. It might be the World's End to him with too many ski apartment blocks down in the town but she was brought up in the mountains there.

When finally he said if ever she really, really needed help, she must come and knock on his door. All she said, her eyes wide open, was "I couldn't ..."

Twenty minutes had passed that evening at 1783 while he was wrapped in these sombre thoughts, edging into depression. The moon was rising. Another ten and he would have to return to the villa. He was cold now to the point of uncontrollable shivering and his foolishness at being out was taking over his thoughts. Then he heard the gentlest of noises in the vines.

Gabrielle was indeed late. Her father had returned early that evening muttering drunkenly that few of his cronies were in the *taverna* because of the holidays and family visits. She could not risk slipping out through the kitchen door while he was snoring in front of the television and had an agonising wait for him to go to bed. She hoped if Ignatio had been able to venture out, he could wait. She knew through gossip in their village he and his brother were back from Switzerland and there was some sort of trouble at the villa. She couldn't believe there were armed men up there.

Feeling her way along the top row of vines her heart jumped into her mouth and she dropped to the ground like a stone. She made out the shape of two men by the old gateway. She saw Ignatio. There was some shouting, an insult or two and her *Piccolino* went limp. The two men had thumped him and picked him up. Her heart was pounding but she kept her head. She knew she must remain low because of the moon and not let her beloved out of her sight.

She followed the party three hundred metres along the wall from the gateway to a big car where another man was waiting. She was panicking quietly but knew if they were taking *Picci* away the only

way was down. The track coming up through the vineyard from the ford was the way she approached the villa and she knew it well.

The jeep rolled slowly forward. There was no time to run on to the villa. There might be a light on in one of the farmhouses in the fields beyond the woods even at that time of the night but they were also too far away. She decided to stick with the car and began to run.

And run she did between bushes and

trees parallel with the track until her lungs hurt with only moonlight to help her. She stubbed her foot against a rock and stumbled, grazing her knees. The ground levelled. She jumped the stream but misjudged its width and landed with a splash that knocked the breath out of her. She turned over in icy water but still had the vehicle in sight.

To her great surprise it crossed the ford and turned into the wood towards her, lurching from side to side. She hid as it passed. Her heart thumped and she wished she was not wearing a light-coloured dress. She couldn't believe a vehicle was driving through woods on steep rocky terrain with only its sidelights on.

Stopping for a moment to catch her breath, she realised it could only be going up to the hunter's hut on the bluff overlooking the ravine. She was frightened now. The cliff had an invisible edge. The whole area was thick with thorny scrub, she was at least five kilometres from the Vespucci estate and ten from her village as the crow flies. It must have been one o'clock in the morning and she was aching, scratched, bleeding and soaked. Above all, she hated herself because she had begun sobbing.

The light from a Tilley lamp in the hut caused Ignatio's eyes to smart after the darkness of the woods. Nevertheless, when the two men unhanded him he drew himself up to his full height. It had been a most undignified ride with his arms held so tightly he thought they would come off. Now his shoulder really hurt but he had the sense to say nothing. When his eyes had adjusted to the glare he saw five men in the old hut all big, mean and ugly. The three who dragged him into the jeep spoke with a guttural Düsseldorf accent. The boss, whom they addressed as *Herr* Kleper was altogether more cultured and polite in his manner and when he spoke, Ignatio relaxed a little.

"*Buona sera, piccolo uomo!* So, you decided on a *passeggiata* tonight," Kleper began in passably good Italian. The grin remained while he mopped his brow. "I have been looking forward to a cosy little chat."

The stone and mortar hunter's hut was shuttered and well-

insulated with straw stuffed above a sagging hardboard ceiling. There was a table and chair on the dirt floor. The only sign of recent occupancy was an empty wine bottle, a pile of rusted shotgun cartridge cases and some charred wood in the fireplace. It could hardly be described as cosy. He and his brother had seen the hut from the far side of the ravine but never ventured along the bluff to find it. The sides of the ravine were too unstable to risk climbing on.

Ignatio's attention turned back to Kleper who had loosened his collar and was rolling up his sleeves. He snapped his fingers and the men hustled him into the chair, binding his wrists and ankles with duct tape with alarming efficiency. Ignatio now focussed on the large zipped leather case Kleper had placed on the table. It was open but he couldn't see what was in it.

"It is very simple, little friend. It could be a problem but I strongly recommend you make it simple. You have documents that do not belong to you. We want them back."

Kleper still grinning, allowed the lid of the case to fall back showing an array of highly-polished surgical implements. They included pincers and grips, pliers and probes and other things Ignatio could not even guess what they were for. He was trying very hard not to.

"I must warn you," he commented bravely, "if I get so much as a scratch ..."

Kleper chuckled, his eyes flaring for a moment. He was close to the lamp, its glaring light tinged with green accentuating his eye sockets and cheek bones. The chuckle was not a natural one, as Ignatio was quick to notice. No sympathy came from anywhere else in the hut. The others maintained their stony silence and Ignatio thought it better he did also.

Kleper selected a pair of pliers from the case and he watched them come at him until he went cross-eyed. Quite naturally he kept his mouth shut. Kleper gripped his nose.

"Open your mouth *Männchen*," he began with more urgency, "just open your mouth. We want the documents. I am the last person who wants to see you suffer but my patience is limited ..."

"We want our money back, *Herr* Kleper," Ignatio blurted, gasping for breath, "and don't think you can bully me ..."

Gabrielle in the meantime had inched her way towards the hut through the scrub in the darkness with courage she did not know she possessed. There were several men inside with her *Picci* but no one outside. A chink of light showed through the shutters. Once again hopelessness came over her. She had no idea what to do. She could only guess *Picci* had been kidnapped and it was something to do with his visit to Switzerland and armed men around the estate.

When he cried out again she stepped back into the bushes, desperate now. The jeep was a little way up the slope. Maybe there was something in it she could use? Petrol came instantly to mind.

"... the documents, the book, where are they Vespucci?"

All Ignatio was aware of was how hard he was breathing, apart from the blood, warm and salty running down his throat. He could not have replied even if he wanted to. Kleper had a firm hold on his tongue with a large pair of pincers. In his other hand was a serrated scalpel he was using as a prod. The stinging sensation made his eyes water and it was all he could do to contain his panic.

When Kleper let go with the pincers with a huff of contempt,

Ignatio's shoulders dropped ten centimetres and in one silly moment he thought he had lived through the worst of the ordeal by standing up to the brute. Typical, he thought, spineless Nazis. No cut-your-throat-as-soon-as-look-at-you here. How wrong he was. What he certainly should not have done was laugh, however nervous it was. Kleper's smile faded and as it did, the hut went cold.

"It would seem there is no alternative. I cannot cut your tongue off, or pull your teeth out. We need you to talk. It must be the pilliwinks ..."

Ignatio's eyes bulged when he saw the next gadget Kleper produced from the case. It was a beautifully-made instrument of brass and chrome as big as a hand. It had a clamp at one end and five rings with a screw key on each and it glinted in the light of the paraffin lamp at every turn. Kleper examined it lovingly, polishing parts of it with a soft cloth. If Kleper was trying to unnerve him again he was doing a good job. Clearing his throat, Ignatio asked, or tried to ask what Kleper intended doing with it.

Gabrielle heard the men laughing suddenly inside the hut and ducked behind the jeep. No-one came out. The vehicle was empty except for holdalls with clothes in them and a jerrycan of petrol. She had worked out the only way she could rescue Ignatio - for this was what she had decided to do - was by causing a diversion. She was trying to figure out how best to use the jeep for this, having rejected using petrol in case it got out of control. In any case she had nothing to light it with.

Another painful cry strengthened her resolve. Until she saw Ignatio manhandled she didn't know how much she cared. She would use the vehicle as a battering ram, to break through the side of the hut. She knew how to drive, the tractor and old van anyway, around the farm.

The trouble was this vehicle was an automatic. The key was in the ignition but only buttons and symbols lit up when she turned it. Frustratingly, there was nothing that looked like a handbrake lever. She closed the door quietly and tried pushing it but hurt her back.

Sitting in the driver's seat once more she told herself calmly she was not stupid, she would work out how to start it then drive it into the hut.

The grin disappeared from Kleper's face when he realised his treasured gadget would not work either on this fellow's little hand. Another good reason Ignatio had not talked, apart from his bravery was because his tongue was now filling his mouth. He was on the edge of consciousness with the heat, the fumes from the roaring lamp, his tongue, painful shoulder and hand with bleeding fingers. At least he had consistently managed to move them to avoid having bones broken.

Images of Dan Dare kept coming in to his head. He wanted to quote the bubbles over the Eagle comic's square-jawed hero and dreamt he was saying it was only an amateur extortionist that didn't have the right equipment.

He did say it and Kleper could not believe his ears. He, a senior *Stalhelm* member being told he was an amateur, by an Italian, in *der englischen Sprache*. His face twitched as he indicated the chair should be moved back from the table.

"Now I have no alternative *il mio piccolo Napoleone*. The pilliwinks must become a *willipinks* …"

There was a roar of an engine outside and tremendous bang. The corner of the hut, the fireplace and chimney and much of the wall with the door in it collapsed in front of Ignatio's eyes. Roof timbers, pantiles and a ton of old straw fell into the room. The table tipped as a beam landed on it. It missed him but hit the lamp. Fortunately, his reflexes sent him backwards to the floor as the lamp base popped, the hut filled with vaporised paraffin and exploded.

Three men were suddenly, desperately trying to stop themselves, their faces particularly, from burning. The fourth had disappeared under the rubble. Kleper was on his hands and knees looking for his glasses, or his precious instruments that scattered as the table tipped. It was just as he stood up the remaining straw and fine dust above him also exploded with a whoosh.

Ignatio was suddenly very conscious and wriggling frantically. He could breath because the few centimetres above the floor was clear of smoke and flames but it was getting lower. He thought he was hallucinating when he saw Gabrielle crawling through the rubble towards him. When she started pulling at the tape binding his wrists and ankles he knew he was not suffering one of the erotic dreams he occasionally experienced during an afternoon nap.

"What kept you ..." he tried to say. He also thought she chose her moments, sprawling across him in the little floral summer dress he liked when his hands were tied.

She did not hear him, or was ignoring him, desperately biting at the tape. She felt her leg burning but freed him and began pulling him by his arms over the rubble. He had momentarily forgotten about his dodgy shoulder and aching hand until then and just wanted to wallow a little longer in his sorry state. Gabrielle, whom he could hardly see now because of thick smoke whispered urgently in his ear "please, please try and crawl. I can't pull you under the car ..."

He did what he was told and followed her beneath the vehicle towards fresh night air. They both stood up outside, coughing and gasping and it was with a supreme effort Ignatio stumbled after her, dodging rocks and gorse. The cold air was the *ceffone*, the 'slap in the face' he needed.

Breathing hard he turned to see a new Mercedes almost buried under half a hut, the whole lot burning fiercely. He was hoping to see people from Düsseldorf he could make an appropriate gesture to but was spun around and yanked behind a rock, unfortunately by his bad shoulder again.

He tried to ask Gabrielle if she had done that, driven the car into the hut but her mind was on matters more urgent. She didn't say she had no idea how powerful it was and she lost control of it immediately she stamped on the throttle. It was sheer luck it glanced off the oak tree and took the corner of the building away. She was able to open the passenger's door and crawl under the vehicle into the hut.

Ignatio mumbled something about saving the family jewels in the nick of time and tried to kiss her but she was having none of that either. It could only have been thirty seconds since they had escaped but two of the men at least, silhouetted against the conflagration were now shouting. Torches flashed in their direction. She grabbed Ignatio's shirt. It was imperative they get as far away as fast as they could through the scrub into the night.

When she stopped finally, Ignatio could hardly breathe. His heart and head pounded. The moon had about set and there was no longer light from the blazing hut assisting their getaway. They had done the last hundred metres by feeling their way through bushes and undergrowth, sometimes on their hands and knees. Now he had a very bad feeling about where they had come to a halt. He sensed a great black void before them from which warm air wafted in ominous silence. Gabrielle whispered in his ear exactly what they had to do.

Ignatio considered himself a good climber. An important aspect of climbing is maturity, a sense of responsibility. When she said they were going down an unknown and unstable rock face exhausted, without equipment, in total darkness both of them black and blue and bleeding, quite naturally he objected.

She turned his face toward hers and said he must trust her. She didn't tell him she could hear voices and had caught flashes of light. He had seen them and was only mesmerised by how they had lit her green eyes, showing her staring at him with great passion. He also saw her dress was torn, her face scratched and bleeding and she or they smelt of paraffin but he acquiesced. Normally he would be ravishing her, in his head. Now she was Mummy.

9/1

It was not until well after midnight that Lucciano realised Ignatio was missing. He noticed lights had been left on and tapped on his door. Then began a panic in the Vespucci household the likes of which there had not been for more than sixty years, actually since Germans last advanced on the estate. On that occasion they were there for an hour and took only food, Cook's Mama said. The villa was of no strategic use to them since there was no easy way north out of the park from the estate.

Clementino shed light on the matter. It was almost impossible for him and his brother to keep secrets from each other. He knew his brother liked the pretty *ragazza* from up the valley. He would occasionally, late in the evening say he was going "cherry-picking," to which Clementino would respond "in your dreams!"

"He will have gone to the old stone gateway in the orchard. That'll be where he meets his girlfriend, when he can," he said as positively as he could to his father without mentioning he had peeked into his brother's diary and seen '1793' on the day's page. That cryptic date didn't take much working out. He had come across Gabrielle and his brother one night sitting by the gateway when he was walking a visitor's dog and thought she was a nice girl with a nice smile, if a little young.

Five of the men who had been posted around the house ran up there. Hector went with them, the best hunting dog on the estate, though they often laughed at him so busy sniffing in the hedgerow he didn't see the hare in the field watching him. After a whiff of Ignatio's jacket Hector ran in a circle then shot into the vineyard and along the wall. He then started down the hill at speed until a whistle brought him back. The Younger had been there and been taken away in a car.

Vespucci was furious, while being partly relieved they were on the trail. He raged at his son's foolishness while also understanding his dilemma at not being able to see his girl and no doubt warn her of serious danger in the vicinity. Lucciano had to stop him going out on his own with a torch. Common sense prevailed and soon he was placating those men around the house who had seen nothing and were very sorry indeed for having let the *conte* down.

Vespucci was most displeased with himself at not having anticipated how ruthless the Neo-Nazis would be in retaliation, or just how determined his son would be at seeing his *ragazza.* This time it was agreed that if Ignatio had not been located by dawn they would call the *Carabinieri* and if necessary, the army, navy and air force.

He had been about to telephone Penny Lane Agency with a message of satisfaction about the exemplary services of their man on the spot for the two-week period. He didn't because he knew he would ask for Wilson to be sent back and he didn't want Miss Lane to think they had muffed the operation the moment their man had departed.

They had their own *armi vincenti,* their 'secret weapon.' It was all around in the form of local people unstinting in their help and support in a crisis. Vespucci knew every one of them. Many lived on the estate and were in his employ. About the Second World War specifically, he hosted a dinner at the villa for the veterans and their families every *Festa della Liberazione,* April 25th. To the older folk in the mountains it marked the end of five years of war, Nazi occupation and twenty years of fascist government in Italy that would never be forgotten.

The men were ready when Cook had finished plying them with a proper breakfast of rolls, salami, ham and cheese. Hot grappa or brandy in the coffee was mostly declined. This was altogether a more important mission. Here were experienced mountain people ready for a search, many already reminiscing past occasions.

Talk was of bad weather, missing lambs and winter blizzards, even though it was mid-summer. Some harped on about events at the end of the Second World War, the derring-do of their fathers and the

Resistenza even though most of them were not yet born. Umberto's father was the acknowledged senior figure in those days in 1943 and 1944 being a member of the *Comitato di Liberazione Nazionale Alta Italia.* He was caught and executed in the next valley. An engraved granite monument to three of these brave *partigiani* marked the place past Carona on the mountain road to the dams and Valbondione. No-one in the villages passed it without stopping to offer their respects.

Lucciano divided the party into smaller groups and with a large map showing the entire *Parco Bergamasche,* allocated search areas as quickly as he could. They knew what to look for, unusual tyre tracks, outsiders' cars, activity around mountain huts. Checking the roads was easy. The valley road south to Piazza Brembana was the only way out of the park.

Speculation on Ignatio's disappearance, snatched probably, was a difficult point to gloss over. Vespucci took the men into his confidence to the extent that it was Neo-Nazi activity relating to unrest in the company that had brought the kidnapping about. He could hardly tell them, or the police, a story of a bank robbery and war-time loan to the Nazis.

They appreciated the *conte* excluding the *Carabinieri* initially. The local man, Pozzi was not in favour because of his keen interest in introducing the very devil into the villages, cctv cameras. He was on holiday anyway. His brother from the south was visiting and they were away on a weekend of their own climbing.

Clementino, under-slept and also feeling responsible for his brother's disappearance, would not be deterred from joining the search. At first adamant Elder was not to leave the villa, Vespucci acquiesced when he saw his son in full climbing gear, with rope over his shoulder. The lad clambered on to the back of the post-War Villaggio tractor Umberto and his brother had managed to start and bring up from lower down the estate. It was ticking over nicely. They had only just upgraded from their 1937 semi-diesel-engined Landini. Thank goodness this one had tyres.

He had a quiet word with Umberto, who understood fully that

Clementino must be watched over. They set off around the back of the villa on their way up to the orchard.

Vespucci changed from an incongruous quilted silk dressing gown, red Fez and matching bow tie in which he had thanked each of the estate workers and their comrades. Now in his shooting clothes at three in the morning he set off in the Range Rover along the flying kilometre to the front gates. His first call was the village. Two of the other drivers were going on to Piazza Brembana, one turning north to Ponte dell'Acqua and the other south as far as the SP27. They would be asking anyone if they had seen a modern car, possibly with German plates, driven at speed perhaps a couple of hours earlier. They would also be calling in at the all-night Agip filling station on the main road.

"Flag motorists down on the local roads, if you have to," he said in earnest.

He covered the two shotguns and boxes of cartridges he had tossed on the back seat. The last thing he wanted was having to explain why he was out before dawn with what could have been construed as a lynching party.

Umberto, his brother and Clementino bumped their way along the track to the orchard and vineyards in the watery light sucking on straws to aid their concentration. Hector was sitting on the tractor's bonnet. Clementino had no doubt now that his brother had gone to meet his girl, a midnight *appuntamento segreto* and that both of them had probably been picked up. He knew the kind of agony his brother was going through and had every sympathy.

A vehicle must have been involved, a four-by-four. The only way they could have got so close to the villa without being seen was up from the ford and through the vineyard. He couldn't imagine kidnappers taking the alternative route, on foot, traversing rocky gullies and thick gorse along the ridge in darkness. It must have been up and down again. There was water in the stream and it wouldn't need a Native American to pick up White Man tyre tracks. Even Hector could do that.

There was the possibility his brother had flipped and eloped. Everyone must have thought along these lines at some time but even he couldn't be that stupid in thinking it was the way out of his problem with his Little Lady.

9/2

Ignatio fell asleep through sheer exhaustion the moment he and Lella were huddled together in a relatively comfortable position after their escape. The early light woke him and he panicked when he realised he couldn't talk and couldn't breathe through his mouth because his tongue was so swollen. Gabrielle told him calmly to breathe slowly and deeply through his nose.

When his breathing was under control he next saw the predicament they were in. They were sharing a patch of moss and dead leaves with a bush in a crevice on a vertical rock face. A slight overhang above prevented them seeing how far they had come down. His girl was scratched and bruised with broken fingernails and bleeding knuckles and he was very sad indeed.

Gabrielle estimated the overhang was ten metres from the top. It had been easy during the night under pressure to descend, feeling for hand and foot holds. She had no idea in the darkness how dangerous the face was and how exposed they were. If they moved they would fall. There was an outcrop of bald rock a little way below them. Beyond that was only cool, damp morning air for a dizzying height to the scrub and rocks far below. There was no sign of life or human habitation in any direction.

As the light improved, Ignatio realised they were on the bluff protruding into the gorge. They had never seen mountain goats on this face and the scrub was so thick at the bottom and top only boar would have rummaged in it for centuries. Following a leader guiding his feet into cracks and on ledges had got him through the pain barrier on their descent. Now his left shoulder and right hand were useless. There was no way he could pull himself back up to the top.

The next time he woke, the sun was glaring. His head throbbed and he was unable to swallow. Lella calmed him by squeezing his good hand and he forgot about their circumstances for a moment with the sweet, smiling face of his beloved. She had stripped branches from the bush to give them more room. She used the twigs to scrape at the soil seeking moisture, fearing it was this above all that Ignatio needed. She had even tried sucking roots but it made her feel sick. It was no good, the ledge, the whole area had been dry for months. She was not smiling at all. Ignatio was feverish.

She knew she could reach the top of the gulley on her own but could not leave Ignatio in the state he was in. The *malvagi* would surely be long gone, though she could not be sure of this. She was really afraid now and her recourse was to sing softly, as she had done many times to her brothers and sisters when they had bad dreams.

"Ninna, nanna, ninna, oh, questo bimbo a chi lo do?
Lo darò alla Befana che lo tiene una settimana.
Lo darò all'Uomo Nero, che lo tiene un anno intero.
Lo darò alla sua mamma che lo ninna e che lo nanna."

'Ninna, nanna, ninna, oh, to whom will I give this baby dear?
I will give him to Befana who will keep him for a week.
I will give him to the Bogeyman who will keep him for a year.
I will give him to his mama, who will cradle him and make him sleep.'

It was with *grazia di Dio* they endured an hour only of morning sun when she heard the sound of a tractor and voices above and a dog barking frantically. The voices were calling Ignatio. She shouted and shouted back. Ignatio heard none of the commotion because he had slipped into unconsciousness. When bright yellow and red ropes like live snakes tumbled down the rock face on either side of them she began to sob with relief.

She was clinging so tightly to Ignatio she didn't notice a rope passed around her waist and fastened.

"Step into the loop *signorina*, stand upright and hold the rope firmly," Umberto said. "You'll be pulled up. *Signorino* Ignatio will be safe with his brother."

She looked around to see Clementino towering over her with one foot on the mossy ledge and one in the blue yonder. Deftly he slipped a body harness over his brother, fastened it, looped the rope through the carabiners and strapped a helmet on him. Now he was also urging her to let go.

"We've got him ... Gabrielle. We'll be back up top in two shakes."

She didn't see the tears rolling down his face as he eased his brother away from the rock face and signalled to the men above to haul them up. He turned away and busied himself banging a piton into the rock, looping a line through it for good measure. He didn't want to waste one of the Ultralite camming devices in his bag, just mark for posterity the spot where his brother nearly came a cropper.

He thanked Wilson silently for insisting they improve their rescue techniques. He might not have managed to get the harness on his idiot comatose brother without those weeks of practice before the robbery.

9/3

It was six o'clock and the ambulance was about to depart from the villa when Cook realised young Gabrielle was exhausted. She swapped Umberto's jacket with her shawl and put her arm around the girl. She had told Umberto how she got Ignatio out of the hut and about their escape. Now she was disoriented and unsure of what to do. Cook had a few words with the *signore* and he went to speak to her.

"Good morning *signorina*," Vespucci began, offering his hand, smiling affably, "I am Ignatio's father. I would be very pleased if you accompanied me to the hospital, the *Ospedali Riuniti* in Bergamo. It would be prudent for you to be checked by a doctor as well as my son. I would also like to thank you for all you've done on this worrying occasion. And please don't fret about the situation at home. I will call on your father this morning to explain the circumstances and reassure him you are safe."

Too tired to appreciate fully what the count was saying, Gabrielle thanked him quietly as he opened the door of the Ferrari for her. As they set off he said they would follow the ambulance and not let it out of their sight. He then asked her name. When she told him, he responded "what a charming coincidence. We have a new biscuit of that name. My sons created it … Ignatio has …"

He was silent for a minute, working the gears as they descended the first of a group of hairpin bends down the valley road. He wondered if the ambulance driver would be driving quite so fast without dark glasses.

Then he asked Gabrielle if she knew the biscuit. Without thinking she responded, "yes, sir, it's my grandmother's recipe …" When she realised what she had let slip, her jaw dropped. The count did not react. He seemed more concerned with keeping up with the ambulance.

"Tell me Gabrielle, do you cook and bake, like your mother and grandmother?"

"Yes sir but I never knew my grandmother. My mother passed away when I was nine."

"So how did you learn?"

"When I was six I wanted to be a cook," she began absently. "When I was seven, I wanted to be ..."

"... I wanted to be Napoleon, and my ambition has been growing ever since!"

Ferdinand completed Gabrielle's quote of the opening lines of Salvador Dali's autobiography. They grinned at each other.

"A more pertinent question if I may, has my son mentioned licensing, royalty, copyright, that sort of thing regarding the biscuit?"

"No sir," Gabrielle said, slightly uncomfortable at the speed with which the ambulance and the count negotiated Piazza Brembana's main street. It was just as well there was no traffic. She was concerned now about Ignatio getting to the hospital in one piece.

"Did you know that Pucci Pasticceria, the Pucci group, has an annual party celebrating, indeed rewarding people for their efforts on behalf of the company? It's a little like the Hollywood Césars ... BAFTAs ... er ..."

"I think you mean The Oscars, sir."

"Ah, yes! Which is why we call ours The Puccis! What I am leading up to is that this would be the appropriate occasion for us to thank you for what I believe this year will be our best-selling biscuit. What do you think of that?"

Vespucci was smiling but had an idea the terror on the young girl's face was real.

"You would have plenty of time to prepare, of course. It is next week ..."

Gabrielle coughed and thought she would choke. Vespucci chuckled and said the ceremony was actually in December and was combined with the company's Christmas party. He apologised for teasing her.

"I should be used to it, from your son."

"I would very much like you to take part in the ceremony. I would like your whole family to come. The company will pay all expenses for a weekend in Milan. Our headquarters are there."

Ferdinand still had the ambulance in his sight as it flew off the Ring Road onto Rue Ruggeri da Stabello, then took a short cut down the cobbled road to the ridiculously narrow *Porta di San Lorenzo.* To give her a breathing space, to get her used to the idea he went on,

"I also insist the company pay for a pretty dress for you, an evening dress, if this is acceptable to you? We would not expect you to have the worry of this when it is we who are thanking you."

"Thank you, sir," Gabrielle responded weakly. Ferdinand realised he needed to tread very carefully.

"But, first things first. I would be very pleased to introduce you to a niece who lives not too far away in Switzerland. Her name is Fabiola, though she will introduce herself as Fabia. She is twenty-two years old, I believe and in the business of fashion. I don't know in what capacity exactly but know she would be delighted to take you shopping and chat with you about dresses and things you would look nicest in. It is what she does best."

He steered away from any mention of money and asked Gabrielle if she had an idea of what she might wear for a special occasion, a ball, a big Christmas party, if there were no limitations to how she could look and dress.

"Ignatio is very kind in leaving, er, with fashion magazines. I enjoy looking at these and day-dreaming but I will listen carefully to your niece."

"So that is settled. There is one more thing ..."

Gabrielle looked at him.

"This year, Ignatio will be announcing the awards. What do you think his reaction would be as he read on the envelope, not knowing you were present, 'the award for creator of our Biscuit of the Year, Gabrielle, goes to ... Gabrielle!'"

Gabrielle opened her mouth but could not speak.

"I think it would be great fun!" Vespucci said on her behalf. "You would then accept a kiss on the cheek from him and the award. This is contained in a red envelope. How much people say is usually dictated by the ensemble rather than nerves! A *'grazie'* is perfectly acceptable. So, young lady, do we have an agreement on this surprise for my son?"

She nodded, smiling until she realised it could also be a disaster in the making. She didn't know how her father would react and said very quietly, "but I don't know ... my father ..."

"Well," Ferdinand began smiling, "I will have a chat with him and indeed, ask him formally for your presence at the ceremony. I will ask that his whole family attend. I'm sure he will be delighted that his daughter is to be thanked in this way."

When they pulled up outside the hospital's *pronto soccorso*, Ferdinand opened the passenger door for Gabrielle. Lucciano pulled up behind them in the Range Rover. He would be at her service, Ferdinand said, until she was satisfied Ignatio was being well taken care of.

"I will leave after seeing the doctor and return to the villa to collect Cook. We will go immediately to see your father about the events of the night. I am hoping he is not an early riser on a Sunday morning? Cook will assure him that we called on you in the early hours because my son had been badly injured and was asking for you. She will say, if necessary, you have at no time been alone with

my son. We have to be both old-fashioned and modern about this. I think we will get away with it!"

Gabrielle bit her lip. Her father did not usually stir until around midday on a Sunday but her absence was a major worry.

"I make breakfast for my sisters first, at about eight," she said absently. She was so tired now she could hardly speak.

"Oh, I'm sure Cook can manage!"

Vespucci took a gold pen and notebook from his jacket pocket and suggested Gabrielle write a note to her father. His lips tightened when she handed it back signed almost identically to the script on his biscuit. He would be having a talk with his son at an appropriate time.

Watching Ignatio being taken out of the back of the ambulance and the wheels on the trolley locking into position, Gabrielle said to the count, "I don't know how to thank you."

"It is I, truly, who do not know how to thank you sufficiently for saving my son's life," he responded.

This time he took her hand and motioned to kiss it with a bow. She blushed deeply.

"Now, let us hurry or we will lose sight of my son. The man, well, the man that you love ..."

Penny Lane goes to Italy

10/1

It took only three days of negotiations on how the German baron and Italian count and their assistants would make the exchange of a briefcase full of rare documents with four suitcases of bonds and banknotes.

Clementino thought it should at least be in a field of maize with Cary Grant and a crop-dusting aircraft in the background, or an Alpine meadow with Julie Andrews and her charges in full song before them. Instead, it was at a MacDonald's restaurant at a deathly quiet Bergamo Airport.

Clementino was told patience and a steady nerve were needed regarding the logistics of moving cash. There is no restriction on the amount that can be moved between EU countries, including Switzerland but it was 10,000 Euros going to or coming from elsewhere. They didn't know where Rothenfelder would be entering Italy from.

"There is also the consideration of the American Secret Service looking for very large movements of US bonds and the *Guardia di Finanza* on a similar quest at all border crossings with Switzerland," his father said. "Eyebrows will be raised if the cases are opened anywhere other than in MacDonald's. They will contain six hundred and fifty million Euros."

Ignatio responded by saying Rothenfelder wouldn't be flying in to Bergamo because they wouldn't want to pay the excess baggage charge on Ryanair. He wouldn't be taking it away with him either because if he was rumbled while leaving the country and couldn't prove it as *bona fide* for tax purposes, forty per cent would be confiscated. He had been doing his own research.

Vespucci knew the exchange would be fraught. Only once had he handed over a case full of money to a stranger as an offer that couldn't be refused for some property and land. Once was enough.

He managed a smile when his youngest said if there was trouble and all else failed he outranked the baron and could do a "don't you know who I am …"

Rothenfelder was seated at a round plastic table in the corner of an otherwise empty restaurant when Vespucci and Lucciano arrived. His assistant was sitting impassively two tables further away, his hat, dark glasses and black leather gloves ensuring anyone else entering didn't come near them.

Four suitcases were discreetly chained to the trolley on which Rothenfelder was resting his hand and foot. The meal on the table had given him huge indigestion and he hadn't even touched it. He was told the coffee was acceptable but the thought of drinking anything from cardboard and plastic only added to his dyspepsia. He couldn't bear to look at the suitcases either, knowing what was in them. It would not be long before he was drumming his fingers.

Lucciano remained outside while Vespucci greeted the baron like an old friend and placed a silver attaché case on the seat next to him. He announced cheerily he would purchase a cup, a carton of coffee and would the baron care to inspect the contents of the case?

On his return, Rothenfelder gave the faintest nod of appreciation.

While they were pretending to talk, Vespucci opened the first of the suitcases on the trolley sufficiently to get his hand in. He did this with all of them, poking around the wads of banknotes. There were bonds to a maximum value of $10,000 and €5,000 and bundles of notes in all denominations including €500, £50 and $100 US. He couldn't help recalling how similar the experience was to the youthful joy of seeing a Picasso box for the first time. These suitcases were more direct in their artistry and over-stuffed.

"Our agreed amount *Conte,* at last night's Interbank rate. As a precaution every five hundred Euro note was checked a second time using a separate scanning method. We have a reputation for thoroughness to maintain. I offer my apologies for an oversight over the promissory note and the unfortunate delay over the holiday period."

Jawohl, mein Hair-oil Vespucci did not reply, much as he might have wanted to mimic his sons. They still laughed when looking through their collection of post-war British comics, of which the Eagle was favourite. He was not so amused the first time he saw Ignatio's crude drawings of the evil, big-headed Klementino floating around on a disc with expletives bubbling from his mouth. Then he remembered the play on words may have come from The Goons and …

"… your apology is accepted, *Baron.*"

He beckoned Lucciano inside.

"And now, may I propose we seal our agreement?"

Lucciano opened a leather case and placed two of eight silver shot cups on the table. Rothenfelder watched him uncork a heavy silver rectangular schnapps flask and top up the cups. He replaced the flask under its elasticated strap in the case.

Vespucci picked up a cup and took a sip.

"Prego!" he gestured to the elderly German. "May the devil cut the toes off our enemies, that we may recognise them by their limping …"

Rothenfelder's Italian was good enough for him to laugh.

"Um die Erfüllung der Vereinbarung," 'to the fulfilling of our agreement.'

They downed the liquor in one.

"Himbeeregeist, to follow our memorable meal at MacDonald's!" Rothenfelder commented with some satisfaction slipping a little padlock key across the table to the count. "And, if I may, I am curious about the engraving on the flask."

"It is actually something for you, *Baron.* We have our differences, our different aspirations but we survive under the same skies. There will always be an ebb and flow, a rising and falling. And with this nautical imagery, may I present you with a silver schnapps flask and cups made by the men of the Admiral Graf Spee for their last commander."

Rothenfelder removed the flask from the case. Beneath a fine engraving of the heavy cruiser in full steam, its *Reichskriegsflagge* prominent, was the inscription *'für KzS Hans Langsdorff, Julfest 1940.'* He looked carefully at the engraving and at the marks on the underside.

"An 800, half moon and crown, Wellner's mark, the *Kriegsmarine* 'M.' How curious, all on such a piece?"

Vespucci understood his questioning this maker's mark on so untypical a piece and so far from Germany with the likelihood it was made with some haste.

"Its provenance is good, *Baron*. It was given to my father by a senior naval officer at the time the loan was effected. He speculated it was constructed from and incorporates the assay mark and maker's mark of silverware purloined from the ship's officer's mess. It is just discernible the marked section has been braised and hammered in ..."

"As *Kriegsmarine* memorabilia goes," Rothenfelder said quietly, giving up his search for a pair of stronger glasses, "with Langsdorff living only another three weeks or so, this is the best and I sincerely thank you."

A young dark-haired woman flitting around the tables looked at the untouched food and asked if they had finished. Her accent was Romanian. She slid what was on the trays into her bin bag and wiped the table, knocking a silver cup accidentally as she did so. Rothenfelder grabbed her wrist. What went through his head belonged to Yesteryear. Catching sight of the Italian next to him eyebrow raised, he let go.

What went through her head, over-worked, underpaid, term fees overdue, what did the old sod think he was doing, was right up-to-date.

"Scusi ..." is what she said.

When he was making things up and sidetracked by comic heroes, Vespucci knew it was time to bow out. He was glad to see the back of the flask but said graciously he thought it fitting it was returned. It was only when the Range Rover was a kilometre away from the airport he settled back in the seat, almost deflating.

He understood his eldest son being perplexed about unresolved moral and criminal issues, particularly the bank's access to customers' private lives and valuable possessions and to entries in a petty cash book indicating unsavoury sources of income. Nevertheless, he might have got to like the elderly German, now surely far, far away from the evil that must have powered his early life. He would follow his own advice to his son. Life is a bumpy ride and you can't smooth it out for everyone riding along with you.

And that it seemed, was that.

"*Himbeeregeist*, Lucciano?"

"*Waldhimbeeregeist*, sir. It was Younger's idea, wild raspberry schnapps. There has been a raspberry motif throughout this business, as I understand it?"

Vespucci tapped the suitcase stowed on the back seat with him thinking cherries would not have had the same bite. He was almost ashamed he couldn't remember the last time his staff, his sons, had received a bonus, just because they were worth it.

10/2

A strange news item appeared in the German popular press at the end of August. Geneva newspapers chose not to pursue it, perhaps because they thought their readership too prudish. Other editors dismissed the story as too seedy and not the type of Silly Season story their readers appreciated.

It concerned a man discovered in a state of distress in the children's play area on Quai Turrettini near Geneva's main railway station in the early hours. He was dressed as a toddler, barefoot, in nappy and pink cardigan with a dummy in his mouth. He was treated in hospital for multiple contusions and lacerations in character with him having received a serious and sustained beating. He had no identification on him and said, when conscious, he didn't carry money around in his nappy either.

A Swiss journalist, Schültz, happened to be at the hospital and recognised the man immediately, Saltzmann from the bank robbed in Zürich at the beginning of the month, Herman's bank. Smutty stuff was not their thing, his editor said with the air of self-righteousness only found in newspaper offices. In any case, the bank story had run its course since there were no new leads on the "Herman, Affair with Sister?" they had ended with. Herman had left the psychiatric clinic and was now being sheltered by the sister in question.

Schültz tipped off an across-the-border colleague in Die Bild. Other popular newspapers picked it up, with glee even, such a story emanating from Switzerland. He then contacted Saltzmann's wife out of curiosity, even compassion and was very surprised she said tartly her husband was not missing. He was away for a couple of days on business. When he described the circumstances in Geneva she put the phone down on him. His compassion evaporated when he realised there was more mileage in the 'Herman' saga and perhaps the most interesting was yet to come.

His first enquiries about Saltzmann in official banking circles were stone-walled, something he was not used to. But then, he was asking direct questions about the banking system and the powerful men who run it. He spent several days on the story off his own bat, mostly in the seedier Paquis district east of Geneva's main railway station. The locals were gearing up for their annual mid-September flea market that had become by tradition a local fête, more street party than flea market.

Schültz soon discovered that *Herr* Christian Saltzmann, the director-general of the bank in Zürich had, it seemed, a predilection whereby he dressed as a baby and had a well-built, middle-aged matron keep him in order along with a lot of other 'big kids.' This perversion was acted out in a local 'Nappy House.' Everyone knew where it was. He couldn't wait.

To his surprise the name *Kinderfrau Greta Windel Haus* was printed next to the bell push on an anonymous apartment block in a Paquis' back street. To his greater surprise when he said he was a journalist from Blick the door buzzed open.

Big, bosomy *Frau* Greta welcomed him in on the fifth floor. Her hair was done in a traditional Bavarian plait. She was wearing a starched white linen coverall and woollen dress to her calves. In the living room of a spacious apartment were toys spread across the floor and a strangely large playpen that was more like a cage. A younger woman was reading a nursery rhyme to a great big, unshaven at-a-guess truck driver. Two others eyed him suspiciously and *Frau* Greta shooed them onto the balcony. Ordinary blokes in nappies crawling onto the balcony set him off giggling.

Frau Greta was not amused.

"A journalist after a juicy story? Well, no luck here young fellow. This is a place of relaxation, where our adult-babies can regress and relax. Absolutely no hanky-panky is tolerated. For the record, no sexual innuendo about age of consent, foreplay, sex games, sex toys, girl toys, toy boys, being on the game, parental interference, child abuse, pre-pubescence, underage girls, child brides, birds and the bees, deflowering, daisy-chaining, sugar daddies, fuck mummies, MILFs or upskirt."

Schültz's eyes opened wide as *Frau* Greta set about preparing coffee. She went on,

"No caning or spanking either. And absolutely no references to breasts, breast-feeding, milkers, mammaries, comforters, teats or nipple substitutes such as cigarettes, though I will allow dummies and bottle feeding. No petting, playing with oneself, 'you show me yours *et cetera*,' cot sharing, bunking or dry humping. No 'dressing up,' lap dancing or playing with fairies. No bighting or talking dirty, squirting or weeing in nappies or of urination of the exhibitionist or Golden Shower type. And no anal play or oral or anal fixation nonsense and certainly no coprophilia or scatophilia. We only take clients who are potty-trained. In short, NO sex, no sexual predilection, fetishes, fantasies, manias, phobias, complexes or syndromes relating to sex."

"So, not much fun here, then!" Schültz blurted out.

Frau Greta cut their interview short saying she really had no time for flippancy. She handed him a list of their services and prices at the door. He got one more question in on his way out, about *Herr* Christian Saltzmann. Matron pulled him back inside.

"I should have guessed your enquiry was to do with Christian.

Yes, one of our clients. It is most unfortunate he went off the rails. We do not condone or provide the extras our clients sometimes ask for but we do have an affiliate who does hotel room visits. I cannot give you her name. I can only guess that Christian's needs were more urgent the other day. Poor man. He did not deserve being driven to this. I bid you a good morning."

Schültz walked down the staircase chuckling. Wondering if Frau Greta was real he asked three woman about to get into the lift if they knew anything about the *Windel Haus.*

"Oh yes," they chorused, "we see Greta and her assistant pushing those bloomin' great babies about in a great big pram every day. If you ask me ..."

"... I will, what hotel do clients go to for something a bit more spicy ..."

The lift door began to close. The women looked at each other.

"... the Paradise ..." was all he heard.

The Paradise *Gasthaus* a block away denied any knowledge of a 'nappy house' or of providing services along the lines Schültz described. It sounded disgusting the Day Receptionist said, her nose in the air. He had to go around the back to find out how the place really worked. It was here with yet more luck that lunchtime he bumped into a woman who would be referred to for the duration of the upcoming story as *"Fräulein X"* only because it sounded better than 'Martha Schmidt.' A nervy, forty-something with a long coat and bag over the crook of her arm *Fräulein* Schmidt did not look like a hotel employee. She didn't look like a Miss Whiplash either, except for her stiletto-heeled boots he could only guess went half way up her thighs.

She gave her vocation away immediately with a retaliatory tongue-lashing after a direct challenge about her 'activities' at the hotel. His bluff worked. She hit him over the head with her bag and tried to run. That was when she was brought to heel, when whip and wig fell into the road and she wasn't going to leave them behind.

Schültz actually treated her to lunch, though not at the station where she said she would be recognised. Trusting she would be named - she paid her taxes, she said - she told him everything he wanted to know about *fesselspiele*, 'BDSM.' Independents like her who didn't work for a studio paid hotel night managers a percentage, as did the prostitutes. That bit of protection was invaluable. Going to client houses or unknown venues with whips and manacles was a no-no, she said, even more than with straight stuff. She was not in the business of fluffy pink handcuffs.

Two hotels kept her bondage gear in trunks and she made a living with a handful of regular clients. Slavery and submission was her speciality. Sometimes clients wanted more Femdom stuff, bondage, whipping or beating down in the basement where cries could not be heard.

"It usually goes back to their private school days, cold, unfulfilled mummies and don't-touch-me-I've-just-had-my-hair-done wives who want the status and money and give little in return. I tell my clients they need to have these wicked thoughts beaten out of them. That's what they want to hear, how naughty they are and how they must be punished. I walk out with the cash."

Saltzmann, she said, looking at a photo of him Schültz produced was just another poor git. She knew him as 'Dummy.' She was not surprised he was a banker. She had seen her bank manager at Manor on Rue Cornavin at lunchtimes fingering knickers in *unterwäsche damen*. She said she was sorry Dummy had been attacked. She didn't do any damage to him, just tickled his fancy. He was in a state about something but she was in a hurry to get the last tram that night.

"I'm not a charity," she said defensively. "If he wants to go wandering off in the middle of the night in the baby gear he likes to wear that's his business. It's a rough neighbourhood. He was probably beaten up for a laugh ..."

The story did find its way back into the Swiss newspapers, upon which Saltzmann's family was not available for comment. The neighbours in Dolder said they were "most upset" by the revelations. The local police chief speaking from outside the Saltzmann residence in a televised interview said the banker was being protected but would not say where, or by whom, or even from whom.

The Silly Season finished but the story went on well into September. Huge sums of money offered to employees of the bank eventually revealed irregularities in its accounting procedures. One said things were so bad only changes in the Constitution would begin to sort out Swiss banking. A formal enquiry handled personally by the very capable president of the Swiss Fiscal Policy Bureau began in the Autumn. The story faded once more, in Zürich.

Continuing interest by Germany's popular press, an altogether more ruthlessly determined machine, uncovered more. Blackmail, extortion, funding of international crime and Neo-Nazi involvement.

Ignatio, following the story, felt avenged and looked forward to the day he read Neo-Nazis were having their tongues cut out, perhaps. Why should such behaviour be one-sided? His young friend stopped him from dwelling on such things. He must not stoop to that same level, she said. It was a matter of rights and law and decency and that allowing such behaviour ...

"... you've been reading them books again!" he said grinning. She threw her arms around him on the bench in the village square and squeezed such he could hardly breathe. One of her aunties nearby smiled. It was alright to do this now, at the beginning of October.

Papa was soon more cheerful than he had been for a very long time. Debts had been paid off, the family name was riding high. An agreement had been reached with the tax inspectorate. He had also quietly made some investments of his own in local projects. There was a long association between the Vespucci family and the city of Bergamo. He had even taken to wearing a buttonhole again when he went out. Cook usually found something for him in the garden and hoped she would soon be ordering from the *fiorista*.

He asked his sons to think about some changes in Pucci Pomodori in particular, perhaps in the feasibility of a continuous production of tomatoes nearer home using hydroponics. He left it to them to present something to the board early in the New Year. Along with the idiom *raining cats and dogs* he had learnt as a student in Oxford, was *why*

154

have a dog and bark yourself? It pleased him realising his offspring were no longer puppies.

He also asked them what they thought of a new company, Gruppo Pucci SpA, the name of which he had been testing. One step back and two forward, was how he described what he had in mind. This was something else he wanted discussed by the board.

The best news of the month was the success of the management buy-out of the Pucci textile business. Biffi and his co-operative were overjoyed with the outcome. It had only happened because Ferdinand agreed to re-invest in the business at least the money the new management paid for it. The name was retained, the Vespucci family had a large stake and Ferdinand made it clear they would take an interest in every stage of its redevelopment.

Other things proposed by a trio of undergraduates from Milan's SDA Bocconi School of Management, including a top *Università Bocconi* graduate that year, were still being assessed. Vespucci had no idea of the demand for specialised materials and the new technological frontiers opening up. There were materials that generated electricity, that communicated with you, carbon nanotubes and graphene ribbons measured in nanometres. The pace was more "fabric your colleagues were proud of last month."

They are already beating the dust out of us Old Carpets, he mailed Evasio, then somewhere between Panama and Hawaii. His brother and *cognata* had purchased a floating apartment and were set to cruise the world at a more sedate pace even than Milan at rush hour. He must be feeling better, Ferdinand thought, because he had already secured an order for refitting the entire cruise ship with Pucci carpets. He advised him to be quick, or think of something else his captive market needed.

Evasio responded with an e-mail telling him there would be nothing to champ at the bit for had it not been for the Old Carpets putting the underlay down many, many years ago.

"Thank you sincerely, Brother for enabling me to rest in peace ... and plan my next career move ..."

One afternoon early in October Lucciano rang up to Clementino to advise him *Signorina* Sophie's car was coming down the drive at speed. Clementino looked with dismay around his bedroom strewn with newspaper, scale drawings, tools, copper tubing, steel plate, pins, bolts and the like. He hadn't let the maid in for two weeks. If he did, he knew the very bit he needed next would go missing and he would have to wait weeks for a replacement.

He had begun work on a one-fifth scale model of the Fowler Supreme he had been mighty impressed with in St. Moritz, before working out his floor would not support a weight of six tonnes or so. He reasoned that even if he got fed up with looking at it, it could be put to use in an outbuilding generating electricity. Lucciano would keep it fired up and watered. Then maybe he wouldn't, so he decided to scale it down further, which is what he should have done in the first place instead of wasting time and money and an already considerable amount of effort, so his brother harped.

Sophie's eyes shone as she came into the room. She didn't seem to notice the area he slept in had been turned into an engineering workshop. He wouldn't have dreamt of doing anything in his studio other than paint and draw. She laid her bag and coat on his bed and did what Gabrielle did with his brother, knelt on the floor before him. That was nice and he was pleased these two girls had met, though they kept a discreet distance from each other. Like Ignatio, Sophie could happily have kissed and cuddled her all day long. She was so sweet, she said. She loved her own little sister to bits. Loving a little sister-in-law would be even nicer ...

On greeting Sophie, Clementino had a choice; to take her rather large hand in both his and kiss it, or simply catch hold of three of her fingers. This she preferred. On this occasion however, she put her arm around his shoulder from her kneeling position and actually kissed his cheek. Clementino went hot and cold.

"My Christmas play," she began, her eyes still shining, "has been accepted for broadcast in the New Year!"

"Oh, how wonderful! That is just ... bloody ..."

"... I came straight away because I will need your help. In the face of all provocation you have remained my best and longest-suffering critic! I would not have carried on with my plays without you as my mentor, my sounding board."

Clementino chuckled about being the critic at the butt-end of the playwright. He knew she had talent and how much of a passion theatre and writing were to her.

"And to celebrate your support over the years, I have a surprise. Papa is still dead set against me having anything to do with theatre, drama, fashion, with anything like that, until he grows up a bit, so I must remain careful. So, I have taken your name as my pseudonym. I am now playwright Clementina Vespuccia!"

Clementino turned away to hide a sudden welling up of tears. He fumbled around under his pillows for a handkerchief. What he pulled out was a pair of Sophie's knickers.

"Now what are you doing with my La Perla knickers, you naughty, naughty man!" she exclaimed.

Clementino, beside himself with embarrassment spluttered she had left them behind in their last art class with her friends. She didn't seem concerned about putting them back on, he said defensively, so he said nothing.

"You naughty man!" she repeated, waggling her finger. "But I have been thinking. I love you dearly, a man who calls me his *raggio di sole*, who does not refer to me as *Girl-Blonde*, or Blonde Sauce, Dumb Blonde, 'raver,' *bionda bomba* or *bimbo* - and I don't know why the English can't get the gender correct. You also know how I love being adored! You can be the guardian of my virginity knickers. Clementina has spoken ..."

Clementino stood there, his mouth open with his Boudicca, his Lucretia, his Zenobia, his *bomba* in front of him, now sitting on the carpet. Pain showed across his face despite her, their, good news and she knew she had thrown him one too many mixed messages. It was time, she realised, for a more solid commitment, a proposal.

"We all have our crosses to bear *preferito*. Yours is *nanismo*. It is not the common achondroplasia. Yours is a metabolic disorder and the reason you have limbs in proportion to your height. It didn't slow your sexual development, thank goodness! You also know you are not alone, with at least thirty thousand people in the United States for example, with some form of dwarfism, most of them with parents of average height. Many of their siblings and offspring are normal height as well. Children are born with dwarfism across the world every day and it is time you put the 'problem' to rest. To us, you and Igno are normal. Well, *eccentrico* but normal! You haven't got to grips with it yet but you are trying. Papa gave me the figures and as you know, he is a *consulente medico* to several countries.

"My problem is being the other way. Yes, yes and that, but being tall I mean. Take it from me you do not want to be tall, loud and clumsy. I get comments about my stature, like you, sometimes as though I'm not there. When I was little, so to speak, it was thought I might have gigantism because my limbs were in proportion as well!"

Sophie stretched her legs towards him, fingering the straps on Valentino platforms that added several more centimetres to her height.

"I thought I was used to it but in Paris last week in a busy street, in daylight, a man just dropped at my feet. I thought he had fainted but he caught hold of my foot and began kissing it at pavement level. What does a girl do?"

Clementino, regaining his composure said she should have kicked him in the teeth.

"I couldn't do that. He begged forgiveness and said he could barely control his foot fetish. It was my feet, my big feet he was captivated by, not a five hundred Euro pair of shoes. You see what I am getting at!"

There was a long silence until Clementino said quietly,

"I wouldn't believe it, if I didn't have a fetish for you myself, every bit of you, that is."

"That is so sweet!" she said. "And what this girl wants to hear! We must strike a deal. You can dress and undress me as the artist wills. Today I'm wearing a cashmere skirt and plain Cervin silk stockings because I keep laddering them. Should you want me to strip, my knickers are the same colour as the skirt in soft stretch tulle net with a lovely floral lace insert that almost covers my *peli pubici.* Tomorrow, maybe the almost sheer toga you like! I'm not shy as you know, so I don't mind just the toga.

"But I am so sorry, my little friend, you can't touch me. I just don't like being touched sexually, even by my girlfriends. In this respect I can only ever be ... your bitch. I can be ... faithful to you ... only on this basis, of artist and model ..."

Clementino flinched as Sophie got up off the floor, this beautiful, statuesque blonde showing silk, lace and cashmere in one not quite graceful movement amidst his oily workshop paraphernalia. His pulse rate increased further as she raised the hem of her skirt slowly up her long, long legs, turned her back to the mirror, made sure her seams were straight and that each suspender was firmly fastened.

"... we have a deal?"

He cleared his throat and replied hoarsely "we have a deal ..."

His tingling subsided when she had gone, a new high sinking to a new low as a fully inflated lilo would if bitten by a shark and dragged under. He felt like a *straccio oleoso,* an 'oily rag.' Even *uno straccio di uomo,* 'an excuse for a man.'

Then he grinned. It could be worse, she could be showing those long legs to someone else. Looking at his steam engine project he realised any beautiful piece of machinery needs the constant attention of an oily rag and burst out laughing. This would be his new motif.

Penny Lane goes to Italy

11/1

Dear Reader, you may be wondering how other things turned out for the Vespucci family after the traumatic events of the Spring and Summer of that year? The Puccis, for instance and whether it was a happy ending for Ignatio and Gabrielle? On what could have been endless mileage in recounting the kidnapping episode, Gabrielle said gently to Ignatio it was inappropriate considering the circumstances and huge family effort put into resolving the problem and saving him, both of them, from the unthinkable.

The sudden deterioration in his condition on the night of his abduction was caused by *setticemia* from the shoulder wound. He was dehydrated and the hospital wanted him to rest and his fingers and tongue to heal. Gabrielle sat by his bedside for four days, reading to him mostly, sleeping in the adjacent room for three nights.

Ignatio was moved by how much she was enjoying her library. He wasn't listening much of the time, preferring to look at her and smile, drop off to sleep and see her again on waking. A nurse brought them, 'the kids,' breakfast. Lucciano took Gabrielle to lunch and dinner every day. He also brought her a change of clothes and books from home that her sisters had packed.

She had a full medical check while at the hospital and was found to be anaemic. They treated burns on her legs and bruising to her upper body from having been thrown around inside the vehicle before it hit the hunter's hut and the air bag inflated.

About her relationship with Ignatio, she asked a discreet question of her *professionista medico* about children and received a discreet but positive answer. They could run tests when it was more appropriate, if she wished. She was very impressed with how thorough the hospital was. She didn't know Ignatio had put her on his medical insurance and asked his medical team to take a good look at her.

161

"She is worth her weight in truffles," he said with some difficulty. "I might talk more sense with my tongue removed but I'm glad she arrived in the nick of time ..."

Gabrielle did know that an afternoon of *trattamento di bellezza* at the clinic within the hospital was his present to her for having broken all her nails keeping him in one piece.

Her father came to take her home. She thought she would have a fight on her hands at his first meeting with Ignatio on the first day at the hospital but he was courteous and sympathetic. He realised, looking at his daughter, there was more to the rescue than the count was letting on but did not make a scene. Cook had driven to the farm every day to prepare meals for the family and Papa said he had got along very well with her. She knew Mama's family and told him they were sad he had lost touch with them.

It was a huge relief her father was complimentary about the Vespucci family and Cook's efforts. They were very classy, he said, very proper, just how people should be, how they used to be. He was also very kind about her own endeavours in the kitchen at home over the years.

Gabrielle almost didn't recognise the old place on her return it was so clean and tidy. Even the yard and rubbish in the shack had been cleared. She was touched they had all made a big effort for their important guests and for her home-coming.

Gabrielle saw *Picci* on several occasions after this with Paolo as her *chaperon* at their aunts' insistence, even though they were not officially courting. At least, there had been no announcement, no proposal. Paolo played discretion perfectly, on one occasion going off to play football with his friends. He trusted his older sister would reciprocate when she was chaperoning him!

She had taken her brother into her confidence about meeting Ignatio at night even though they would both have been in big trouble if Papa had found out. If anyone was up late with her, it was Paolo. She stressed they did nothing wrong. He knew, he said. He was more concerned about her being out in the mountains at night and had

once come looking for her. She was sorry she worried him to this extent and after this let him know where she was meeting *Picci* and when she would be home, waking him if necessary on her return.

For two and a half weeks during October, Ferdinand's niece Fabia hauled a very lucky Gabrielle and her brother around the fashion weeks of London, Paris and Milan. Fortunately it tied in with *Picci* having to catch up on work, apologising he would not be able to come over until the end of the month. Gabrielle left the responsibility of looking after everything to her next eldest sister. Her father assured her they were on top of things and would cope.

The extended trip grew from the original idea of Fabia taking Gabrielle to Milan to look for clothes for the Christmas awards ceremony. Ferdinand asked his niece if the two young ones could accompany her through Fashion Week. Having met Paolo, Fabia said she would be delighted, if they didn't mind a hectic schedule. Ferdinand stressed he wanted them all to have a jolly good time and that it should be a memorable experience for a young woman he believed would soon be part of the family. Fabia got the message.

They landed at London Heathrow and after a frenetic day in Oxford Street, Kensington and Chelsea by request for some sight-seeing and a little shopping, they took the train to Berkhamsted in Hertfordshire for two days at Champneys. Gabrielle's eyes opened wide. She didn't think anything could top the facial and manicure she had at the Bergamo hospital beauty clinic. This was how the trip started.

A dress for The Puccis was made for her the following week in Paris by a new designer, Jakko. He tutted every time she walked in to his studio in the 2nd *arrondissement,* reminding her she must stand and walk with a straight back. Nevertheless, he had enjoyed the challenge he said, with a mock wiping of his brow. He gave final instructions to his seamstress, his mother, without using pins on the most delicate of materials.

Gabrielle was ecstatic as she looked in the mirrors at a person she only dreamed she could be, in a dress of overlapping squares of black charmeuse silk. It was so light and clingy and moved with her perfectly. They had followed its progress from Jakko's sketches to him showing how to cut the material on the bias.

The dress was a special favour for Fabia. It was expensive with the quantity of silk he was using, he said dismissively but it emulated the sumptuous nature of the Senate at Rome and Legions returning home with plunder, including black slaves like himself.

Each time they called at his garret studio in rue d'Aboukir Gabrielle hid behind her brother giggling, looking at the young Mauritian constantly preening hair that looked like a pineapple. He was nearly as funny as her *Picci.* She didn't think he was gay because he had propositioned her. Then she wasn't sure. He said he expected she had a handsome hunk, a *bell'uomo, un bellâtre,* for her big night. Her proud response was that her *ometto* was her prince and a very big character. Jakko agreed that was what counted.

About the dress, Gabrielle never did get to learn the cost of the "favour."

The pace did not let up in Milan. The fashion shows there were as meticulously organised with racks of clothes and accessories bagged and labelled for each model. In the city's *quadrilatero della moda* Fabia introduced Gabrielle to a completely different way of shopping for good quality clothes. Here were discreet designer outlets in unmarked garages, basements and inner courtyards with a number or logo on the bell push. Many were not obviously shops. You had to be in the know.

It was in a small shop off Via Montenapoleone that Gabrielle spotted the most beautiful shoes she had ever seen. A heel broke, to her immense embarrassment as she walked awkwardly across the floor. Two more pairs were boxed up. She would practice walking in them at home trying very hard to walk and stand straight as well. Fabia didn't tell her the price of these items either.

When the Milan week finished she couldn't wait to get back to her family and animals and silence of the hills. She would not forget the glamour and excitement and seeing professional make-up, hair people and dressers in action. If she had been taller, one said, she could have been a star on the runways, The Face, The Look, whatever she wanted ... She didn't believe a word of it but had never felt so good in her life.

She blushed when she had to walk across a highly-reflective floor even though Fabia had bought her some really beautiful new underwear. The models, such attractive boys and girls, took no notice of the floor whatsoever. How she wanted to share her experiences with *Picci*. And how difficult it was to keep the secret.

Two very tired young Italians could not thank Fabia enough at the end of the month. She reported to her uncle it was so sweet, their joy at everything from Grenadier Guards at Buckingham Palace to busy catwalks at Covent Garden, to the traffic around *L'Étoile*, an outdoor fashion show beneath the Eiffel Tower and a night at the opera in Milan as a last treat.

Paolo returned to school with a new confidence after his "international fashion assignment," as his father had explained it when requesting time off for his son. It was granted readily when the headmaster heard it related to the Vespucci family. They all looked forward with keen interest to a full report on the assignment, he said.

Gabrielle and Fabia were to return to Milan in December for one more round, looking at coats and accessories. *L'Immacolata Concezione* on the eighth day signals the start of Christmas in Italy that lasts to January 6th. The Puccis were almost upon them.

Gabrielle took Fabia's advice on a Miu Miu clutch bag but was uncomfortable with the cost of a trench coat by the same designer. They were still within budget Fabia replied deftly to her concern about prices.

"I've seen such beautiful people and beautifully-made things over the weeks. It's not real that I have some of these things. Every night, when everyone is asleep, I unwrap something from its tissue and want to cry it is all so lovely."

"Looking good is very real!" Fabia responded. "You start as you mean to carry on. I will let you into a secret today because coats are expensive items. Firstly, it is getting colder and you need one. *Picci's* father authorised me to put one on the company account. Secondly, your appearance will cause a sensation. You will look sensational. You will forget price tags ..."

"... I will be brought back to Earth by my sheep!"

They went into a fit of laughter, drawing attention to themselves in a shop full of otherwise demure ladies.

Gabrielle and Ignatio enjoyed briefly the Italian tradition of having a moral guardian, fifteen-year old Paolo, trailing them. It wasn't long before Ignatio was coming over twice a week to the farm and they would walk out on their own. He even helped with the sheep in rain, then in the first snow to fall in the mountains. No-one tutted, no ladies in black even. Old ladies were young once and not that long ago, in their heads, the aunties agreed. *Picci* was utterly charming and entertaining and could have got agreement from them on anything.

She did meet him on two very cold late-night occasions at 1783 and 1894 and they agreed it was neither appropriate nor necessary to do it again. Meetings alone were ironically harder, more intense. Now they were planning, not just dreaming. Ignatio said his being able to call on her was the start they had waited so long for.

How hard she found keeping *segreto* the events of recent weeks, the places she had been jetted to and driven around in a limousine to see. She would remain steadfast with her promise of secrecy about

The Puccis to Ignatio's father. Not to was unthinkable. She knew their future relationship hinged on this and she was exceedingly careful. Her father, brothers and sisters were all solidly behind her in this.

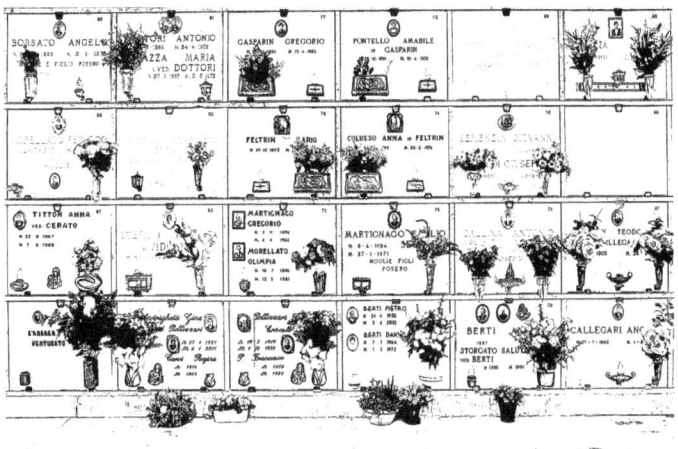

November 1st in Italy is *Ognissanti,* All Saints' Day and a public holiday. Further south it may be the day on which to catch up on the veneration of saints that had been missed during the year. For the Vespucci family, November 2nd, *Commemorazione dei Defunti,* All Souls' Day was more important, though still not in a Catholic sense. The entire household and many visiting relatives walked down to the village, to the tiny chapel, to remember Mama particularly, with flowers.

Gabrielle's family did the same a few kilometres away. That was a sadder occasion. Only Gabrielle and Paolo remembered their mother who had died of a chest infection in a particularly bad winter. It was an emotionally trying time for their father and it had fallen on his eldest daughter for some years to cheer them up, especially at supper on that day, with biscuits and other treats.

That year would be a difficult one because Ignatio had invited her to supper at the villa. "Delightful idea!" his father responded when he asked. "She is a nice young woman to have around." Ignatio missed his father's subtle acknowledgement of her as a daughter-in-law.

She was in a quandary. She really wanted to come but asked if it was appropriate as a first occasion. And should she wear black? Black and orange and a *cappello da strega*, a "witch's hat" maybe, Ignatio said. They turned it into more of a humorous occasion at the villa with just a touch of the macabre. He didn't tell her he had the perfect accessory if she needed it, an authentic *cappello corte di buffone*, red and yellow with large bell.

All of them cringed at the mention of the alien Halloween but admitted to leaning towards it. They preferred the traditional celebration of the deceased with the bounty of Autumn. Big orange *zucche* were already decorating steps and window ledges and if the occasion could be spooked up a little with tales of ghosts and odd happenings on misty nights around the mountains, so much the better.

Ignatio came up with the idea of Gabrielle and he preparing some treats for her family by way of compensation. This was to accompany a pumpkin she had made into a face and a pasta dish Paolo said he would like to have a go at preparing in her absence. Ignatio had really been looking forward to showing Gabrielle where he worked. They would deliver the goodies and return to the villa. The Trabbie wasn't quite ready, he wanted an authentic East German army camouflage paint job done on it but it only took a moment to fit the pedal extenders to the Range Rover.

He had closed the door to his bedroom for propriety. When he told her he didn't think it polite for a young lady to see it she told him not to be so old-fashioned. She teased him mercilessly for the next half hour.

"Please let me see your bed ... where you sleep ... where you keep your clothes ... where your nearest bathroom is ... *per piacerissimo!* 'pretty please!' Let me see where you dream about me ..."

He gave in, of course. She was already well impressed with his laboratory kitchen and roof garden and at how immaculate and beautiful and big it all was. She gasped as he opened his bedroom door.

"Your bed and your furniture is so splendid. And you have your own bathroom!" she exclaimed. "We have one bathroom for seven of us and the *latrina*. And you have a whole room for your clothes! I keep my *biancheria* in a cardboard box, otherwise my knickers get mixed up with my sisters' ..."

She started giggling. Not at that but at a full-size car hanging from the ceiling in a corner with a rather dusty Noddy about to fall out of it. She turned to him eventually and said it was the most beautiful bedroom she had ever seen.

"A *castello* for my *ragazza* ..." he reminded her.

At the villa on the evening of November 2nd, Ignatio intrigued everyone by laying a large parcel down the centre of the dining room table. It was wrapped in white linen and tied with string all the way along. Surely, Gabrielle thought, he had not intended it to look like a shroud? He came into supper carrying a long willow frond. She found out what it was for when she prodded the linen gently and her fingers were tapped smartly from across the table.

"*Il rispetto per i morti, si prega di ...*" he said grinning.

Their traditional autumn fare that evening was *gnocci con porcini*, pasta with a ham and chestnut filling, *risotto con la zucca* looking very colourful served in pumpkin shells, roast potatoes and chicken with a truffle sauce. There was a huge white truffle in the centre of the chicken dish. Gabrielle had never seen, or tasted one and was grateful that *Picci*, hopping up and down from his seat, wanted to serve her. His father laughed at one point, telling him to leave the girl to eat.

She said it all looked and smelled so good she didn't know where to start. The truffle made the chicken dish divine. It was the most extraordinary transformation. Lucciano was *tartuffi* master. He knew where to find the *porcini* too and if she asked, he would give her some sauce and peelings to take home.

At the end of supper Ignatio untied the parcel. There was a collective groan from around the table as a complete skeleton made from almond and hazelnut meringue was revealed.

"Fammi il piacere! 'Give me a break!'" he said "This year, a superior *Ossi di Morto biscotti* instead of the usual pile of dry bones. It took a month to make!"

Religious only when it really mattered, Gabrielle prayed that night with thanks that her brothers and sisters and father enjoyed Paolo's *pasta con la zucca,* the girls' contribution of muffins she had taught them how to make and the *Picci Pasticceria* she and Ignatio spent the morning preparing in his amazing penthouse kitchen. She thanked Fabia for the items of clothing she lugged back to Fóppolo from Fashion Week, saying modestly, they would come in useful.

She was most grateful her dinner with three titled gentlemen had gone so nicely. Terrified to begin with, she was soon laughing about the odd things they said and did, such as dining by candlelight with fake cobwebs around them and Lucciano appearing and pulling a string to animate paper bats. He was wearing evening dress also and was sporting a set of tombstone teeth. It was such a contrast to the sombre occasion it was for her family.

They are definitely not normal, the Vespuccis, her aunties whispered. She knew they were extraordinarily kind and thoughtful and really quite funny at times.

11/2

A week before Christmas and the night before The Puccis, Gabrielle's family were taken to the Meliá Milano where they would be staying for the weekend. Gabrielle, her father, three brothers and two sisters stood gaping at the tapestries, marble flooring, white staircases and pre-War racing car in the foyer. Dinner was included that evening, as was lunch the following day and a buffet reception after the awards ceremony. All the hotel's facilities were available to them courtesy of Gruppo Pucci SpA.

"You could fit the farm into this place!" Gabrielle's father whispered at dinner. All of them felt a little incongruous in the dining hall and were sure waiters were watching their every move. The younger girls discussed in earnest which knives, forks and glasses they should be using. The boys marvelled at the way the table was laid and how the food on each dish was presented. Paolo said he expected nothing less from Sis after this and after the things Cook and Ignatio had made especially for them.

Towards the end of dinner, *Signor* Farangio told his family to finish their mouthful and make sure there was something in their glass because they were going to offer a toast. The younger children watched their papa carefully.

"We've never done a toast, as a family," he said. "It means we are going to thank someone or congratulate them. Any guesses who this evening?"

"Facciamo brindisi Papa ..." the youngest piped up innocently to much laughter.

"No, no, bambino! Tonight it is a toast to Lella, a wonderful daughter, sister, friend and Mummy!"

Dad put his arm around daughter and told her there was no need for tears. He thanked her for how she had looked after them all over the years and above all how she had put up with him, particularly over the matter of the Vespucci boy. She in turn thanked him for allowing her to go to England and France knowing how much extra work those weeks had placed on everyone around the farm.

Paolo, seated on the other side of his father, all ears, stood up as his father had done and said,

"I would like to offer a toast to *Sorella Maggiore* as well, not only for putting up with Papa ..." his father pointed a finger at him, grinning, "... but because she has done us proud tonight. And tomorrow she'll do us proud again with an award. And I got driven around in a limo in London, Paris and Milan, got some flash new clothes and saw loads of real models! And the opera was fantastic!"

His father responded with a proud *"bravo! bravo!"*

As the company's do was getting under way the following afternoon at Rho-Pero north-west of the city, Ferdinand slipped out and drove the few kilometres to the Meliá Milano on the edge of town. He wanted to shake hands with every member of the family before his son's big surprise. The children remembered him doing magic tricks while Cook prepared breakfast for them on the morning Ignatio was taken to hospital.

Signor Farangio was moved at how thoughtful the count continued to be in coming over to the hotel. In long johns and with a thumping head had not been the ideal state in which to meet an aristocrat for the first time. Now he was determined he would be a father his daughter was proud of.

"I ordered some Dom Pérignon, on my account, *conte*," he said as the waiter appeared, "hoping we would be able to thank you for your generosity with this hotel and everything you have done for us."

"This is a very kind gesture, *Signor* Farangio," Vespucci responded. Gabrielle, Paolo, their papa and he clinked glasses. Farangio knew a good Champagne when he tasted one but still preferred his brother's best *prosecco.* He said nothing and had two sips only, not needing to be reminded how important this occasion was for his eldest daughter.

Vespucci sat briefly next to Gabrielle. Her dress was perfect he said and gave the impression of a very feminine centurion going in to battle. He had not even been primed to comment along these lines. She was wearing a small gilded, red ceramic flower in her hair with a matching adornment dangling from a tiny leather bag. He took her hand briefly in his, such a pretty girl he thought. It was good the younger ones were being given the spotlight.

He said something to that effect to Gabrielle. He also said it was on occasions like this he missed his wife's company, her presence.

"It is because of the joy you are about to bring to my son that I want you to accept a piece of jewellery that belonged to his mother," he said quietly. "It has special significance to me, of course. But it has no significance when shut away in a box."

Gabrielle opened the white leather case and was stunned. Here was a bracelet of platinum and coloured diamonds, he said. Each diamond was set in an exquisite floral mount. Ferdinand took it out of the box for her and fastened it around her wrist.

"Just perfect, an exact fit."

Gabrielle put her arms around the count's shoulders and touched his cheek with hers, whispering she would try and live up to it. Her father's eyes nearly popped out when he got a good view of it sparkling against his daughter's dress and the count's dress suit. He stood up and began clapping spontaneously, saying,

"My daughter looks like a million dollars tonight and is probably wearing another as well!"

Gabrielle carefully unclipped the red flowers from her hair and bag, first seeking reassurance from across the table. Fabia knew what she was about to do. Gabrielle turned to her twelve-year old sister, also as pretty as a picture and clipped the piece into her hair. She was overcome and rushed out to the mirror in the hallway. The second piece she gave to her eight-year old sibling from whom there was a similar reaction.

When the chauffeur appeared, the whole family filed into a stretched limousine. Snow had begun to settle, across which coloured lights from many beautiful shops around the hotel were already making this a night Gabrielle would not forget. Twenty minutes later at the rear of Pucci headquarters they were shown into a deserted office near the main hall from which they could hear talking, laughter and music.

It was only then, after weeks of preparation and excitement that Gabrielle began to tremble. It turned into an outright shaking until Fabia reminded her calmly how models at fashion shows cope with photographers, television cameras, the occasional histrionics, a fall maybe and the great, the good and the highly critical looking on.

"Hold your head level and walk positively down the runway without taking your eyes of your goal and your mind off the purpose of your entry."

Hiding behind the curtain of the makeshift stage she began to relax at the laughter through the proceedings. Ignatio was funny and she was so proud at how easily he controlled the crowd. She had not seen him with so many people in this way.

She stepped into the wings and took a deep breath as he said,

"Now we come to the last part of the ceremony, that of our best-selling product. This year it is a biscuit, the first in the *artigianale* series we think will become very important to the company. So, the prize for our Biscuit of the Year, Gabrielle, goes to ..."

He pulled the card from its gold-lined envelope and paused. His eyes searched the hall in disbelief. When he saw Gabrielle at the edge of the temporary stage, so close, he gasped.

It was with a big smile she did what had been advised and strode across the stage as confidently as a seventeen-year old can, as Ignatio just managed to finish his announcement into the microphone with a strangled "Gabrielle." He was so overcome at the sight of his *ragazza*, his *giovane donna* in a silk evening dress, red shoes with heels and diamonds around her wrist he pulled a large handkerchief from his breast pocket and dabbed his eyes. She put her arm around him, genuinely concerned and kissed his cheek.

The clapping turned into cheering. Without taking her eyes off her *Picci* she kicked off her shoes and knelt facing him on the stage with her hands in her lap, as she had done almost since they had met. The cheering got louder. Ignatio almost got control of himself, stuffed the handkerchief back in his pocket, gestured towards her with his hand and croaked into the microphone,

"How can I not love this beautiful young woman ..."

That brought the house down, or rather, to its feet with whooping, whistling and applause. The chanting began, "Min-i, Max-i, Min-i, Max-i ..." proof the rumour was correct, that this was how the work force referred to him and Clementino. Then glasses were raised as the couple touched hands.

The chanting changed to the more personal and just as surprising "Ig-no, Tin-o, Ig-no, Tin-o ..." as Ignatio went through a mock scolding of himself for forgetting to hand over an envelope and small box to the winner of their most important award. Gabrielle stood for this and in stockinged feet now, opened her arms to Ignatio's brother who appeared, giving him a kiss on the cheek also. The noise did not stop.

A man might hold a woman gently by her shoulder under such circumstances. She wasn't sure if it was absolutely correct but she drew both brothers to her side in this way, to her breasts. She didn't let go of them, even when she saw the photographer fiddling with his camera and flashgun against the hullabaloo. She remembered Fabia's sassy advice "just go for it, Girl! Say yes to everything ..."

11/3

Christmas Eve had been a mute affair at the Vespucci villa for some years. Not so that year. The house buzzed, people came and went all day wishing the family a *buon Natale.* The Farangio family arrived during the afternoon as guests of the Vespuccis. They would be there until *Salutando l'Anno Nuovo.* Their neighbours were feeding the sheep, cats and budgies. On their arrival Ignatio noticed immediately the youngest children were clutching a book each, obviously having been allowed to bring one with them by *'Mama.'* They were all from Gabrielle's library.

Farangio's new suit was courtesy of his eldest daughter and he felt good as he entered this grand house, he told her, about being smart again and not going up to the *taverna* so much. He was done with that. He also said he did not want to miss one more moment of his daughter at home before she was married. Gabrielle blushed, ticking him off for intimating such a thing. She would be home a while yet, she said. She had no idea what was coming.

The children were in awe of the house, as they had been of the hotel. A decorated tree to one side of the staircase reached up past the first floor. On the other side was the *presepio,* the 'Nativity scene,' the most beautiful they had ever seen. The principal figures were arranged in a tiny village of terracotta made, Paolo suggested, to look like Bethlehem. Tiny lights showed in some of the houses.

Some of the figures, Vespucci told the children, were hundreds of years old. There were many more in storage. All of them had their name written underneath and every Christmas they had great difficulty in deciding which of the figures and animals should be shown.

"We are not a religious family," Vespucci admitted quietly to *Signor* Farangio, "a shortcoming Cook and her relatives reprove us for every year. But tonight because your children are here, my manservant and some of his relatives will be dressing up as shepherds to play and sing."

Farangio thanked Vespucci copiously. He asked the count if he minded them keeping a Christmas Day tradition going, of the children putting little notes under his plate to be read out before supper. Vespucci said his boys had not done that for a very long time and he would be honoured to hear the children paying their respects to their papa.

On Christmas morning Gabrielle's three brothers perched on the tractor with Ignatio and set off around the estate with a trailer stacked with hampers bouncing about behind them. They did the deliveries in double-quick time laughing all the way. It was predictably mostly at Big Sister's expense but it was clear they adored her.

Umberto handed Ignatio a bottle of his home-made Grappa, reminding him it was very strong but that he might need it that week. His wife waved a packet of Gabrielle biscuits offering congratulations to Ignatio and his beautiful girlfriend. All three boys chorused "that's our sister!"

Forty people would be seated for Christmas lunch. Before Cook and her sisters were ready to serve, Gabrielle was sitting near the log fire with her arm around her father and youngest sister. The rest of her siblings were about, somewhere. The log was huge and took four men to carry in. It was one of the Vespucci traditions, endeavouring to keep the *Ceppo di Natale* alight until New Year's Day. Her papa was looking forward to lunch and yet more fine wine, including a 1967 Brunello di Montalcino and 1974 Barolo he had seen in the kitchen and was eagerly waiting to taste.

The red envelope Gabrielle received at the award ceremony contained a cheque that meant little to her as she did not have a bank account. She wanted her father to have it to help with household bills and some of the expenses around the farm that were a constant worry to him. That was a few days earlier

His mouth opened. It would do more than that, he said, looking at her wide-eyed. There was enough to clear his overdraft, buy a new van and a new tractor and pay off the mortgage on the farm. He was really chuffed being invited in to the bank manager's office with a Vespucci cheque to be told his overdraft would be extended. He had, in effect, a new credit facility. There was no need to wait for it to clear.

It was a different family that went off shopping in Bergamo the day before *vigilia di Natale*, Christmas Eve. This time they were there for some serious shopping.

The small box Gabrielle received at The Puccis she brought with her to the villa. It contained a plastic novelty item with pink feather, one that unfurled and squealed when blown. The piece of paper it was wrapped in was written in English and she called Ignatio over to ask if he could translate it.

"How to insult your father-in-law without him realising," he translated, cautiously.

The next lines he read in English,

"Tickle your arse with a feather! ... What did you say? ... Particularly nasty weather!"

Then Italian,

"*Solleticare il culo con una piuma! ... Che cosa hai detto? ... Clima particolarmente brutto!*"

It didn't make sense, he said. Gabrielle's father guffawed and Ignatio looked to him for explanation. It was *Signor* Farangio who surprised everyone, drawing their attention in rather good English to the alliteration of the original language. Gabrielle had two heroes that Christmas Day she said, two who would never be bettered.

Ignatio asked Gabrielle's father politely where he had learnt his English. Bashfully, he replied he was an Elvis impersonator. He had learnt English from song sheets. Gabrielle's younger siblings stifled a giggle.

"No," eldest daughter began firmly, "Papa is rather good. He even has costumes and is well appreciated at social functions."

Signor Farangio preened.

177

"Fantastic!" exclaimed Ignatio. "You must do an impersonation this evening after supper. Of all the musical items tonight yours is one we couldn't possibly miss. We'll pop up to Fóppolo and get your kit. If it makes you feel more comfortable, I'm doing Paul Robeson ..."

He breathed a sigh of relief at having got his boots back on the correct feet. He also knew his secret with Lella's father was still a secret. He would not be 'doing' Paul Robeson and he had known for days about Lella's father's Elvis impersonation.

Sophie arrived later that afternoon after her family's Christmas lunch. Clementino took her up to his studio, to show her his etchings. Being alone together was something that had become more frequent in recent weeks. They sat at his drawing board on this occasion giggling. He was wearing her present of man-about-the-estate Wellingtons in his size, green, with thick yellow soles that laced at the top. He had been searching for a pair all year. She was wearing his present of a heavy silver chain around her waist and had promised solemnly she would take it off only under an "exceptional circumstance" and that this didn't mean taking a bath.

They were better friends of late since she had 'taken his name' and their relationship clarified. Her *sceneggiato radiofonico*, her drama, was also going well in rehearsal and was on schedule for broadcasting in January at peak viewing time on *Befana*, the Feast of Epiphany, the day Italian children traditionally receive presents. The play was called *Befana e le sue scarpe nuove*, 'Befana and her New Shoes.'

A television producer had taken her out to lunch, intrigued by the play and interested in what she may be able to contribute to a planned new television drama series. There were many in the industry so, so tired of nubile *ragazze* prancing around to pop music on daytime television, he said. Sophie was learning discretion. She didn't mind it at all but didn't say it.

Clementino and 'Clementina' had also teamed up at the beginning of December to produce a series of anarchic Christmas cards. Clementino had finished colouring the first six drawings, the etchings, ready for printing. The plan was to build up a stock for the following year using material left over from regular print runs, when the printing office was quiet and when Papa was not in the building.

The artist featured himself in the first, in a green costume and hat with distinctly slanting eyes, seriously burdened with a huge sack. The caption read,

"Made by Elves in China ..."

Ignatio's mate Tel suggested they do something on the theme of "Elf and Safety" but they didn't understand what he was on about.

The drawing that really set them off laughing that afternoon was Sophie in her little sister's ballet costume and shoes. She was holding an LED wand. A similarly contemporary halo rigged up over her head had slipped. She had not been happy suspended for an afternoon by a rope and harness, her legs spread, over the very tip of a fir tree that disappeared up her tutu. Clementino had caught her displeasure and decided after much agonising to include the tackle in the drawing.

Of many possible captions, they settled on "Christmas is a Pain in the Arse."

It had taken Clementino a long while to realise that Sophie loved dressing up. Obvious really, for a frustrated model and drama queen. He was yet to spring on her his newest plans for her as his model. That would be a New Year's Eve surprise. He would do a cartoon series of her as an 'undercover' *Carabiniere* getting into a scrape in each episode in which she lost most of her clothes. It was right up her street.

In a stroke of originality, he thought, he would call the misfortunate young woman Jane, as in the English 'Plain Jane' because she certainly was not. He mulled over *Comandante* Clementina then settled on *Capitano* Pucci. The *Carabinieri* motto *Nei Secoli Fedele,* 'Faithful through the centuries,' was coined for her. She would make her debut in the firm's rather dry monthly journal, Pucci Matters, he intended to revamp in the New Year. That should increase circulation and therefore interest in what the proposed Gruppo Pucci SpA were up to. It might even make a national daily. Hopefully one her father didn't read.

Vespucci came across his son *in flagrante* in the middle of December in the print shop with his sketches for the cards but did not comment other than shake his head slowly. It was to Clementino's surprise just afterwards he asked if he might have a single, hand-drawn version of 'Christmas Fairy.' Clementino obliged and watched his father address the envelope 'Miss P. Lane ...'

Vespucci had just received a card from Barbados adorned with coconuts and exotic flowery hats. Penny was out there early, with friends, because at Christmas she would be back at the grindstone. The same old pain, she wrote, though she would face it refreshed and with a tan. Their coterie, already known on that island paradise as the Liverpool Ladies, had sampled the authentic Caribbean Punch and wanted to offer Vespucci and his family a toast to their success and best wishes for the future. Her team in Liverpool, she reiterated, was ever at his disposal.

It was fortunate the card made him laugh because in the same post was the Agency's bill for their services during the summer.

Penny Lane goes to Italy

POSTSCRIPT

Christmastime or not, the last word of any story in which The King is mentioned should go to him. To Elvis that is, not the Baby Jesus.

Ignatio had telephoned Gabrielle's father shortly after The Puccis and driven up to Fóppolo in his Trabbie to meet him at the *taverna*. The car performed well in reverse, though there was no back-tracking here. Still along military lines he was giving serious consideration to restoring a British Humber Pig Armoured Personnel Carrier for more difficult situations, as the one he was driving to.

The meeting was nothing to do with Elvis impersonation since Ignatio had yet to learn about *Signor* Farangio's talent. He was on the time-honoured quest of a young man seeking permission from the father of the girl he loved for her hand in marriage. *Signor* Farangio was very impressed with this young man in particular venturing into a bar that could sometimes be a difficult place for a big bloke to survive in.

When the regulars that evening twigged he was there to ask Farangio for his daughter's hand, it was as though someone had pressed 'mute.' There was real interest. Even the clinking of glasses ceased briefly. Farangio didn't say a word for an awfully long time after Ignatio popped the question, so to speak. Then a grin appeared across his face.

"Marrying my daughter means you take on the back end of your estate, including us *beoni!* If you are prepared to do this, then you have my respect and permission of course, to take my girl away. But don't forget, if you don't look after her good, you will have all us ugly buggers to contend with. We have a deal ..."

"... we have a deal," Ignatio agreed hoarsely.

The 'ugly buggers' broke into spontaneous clapping and some murmuring, to be countered by Ignatio saying he would buy a round of drinks for everyone.

"Do we call you sir ..." one asked pointedly.

"Does he have big prospects?" one old woman cackled without taking the pipe out of her mouth.

"Just shut it," Ignatio said grinning, "I can't help being a *nobile dei conti di Bergamo* but call me that and drinks are on me for the rest of the evening!"

"Oo, thank you ... *nobile* ... sir!" came the response.

"You can also call me Igno. That way, I'll know you're being genuine. It's my brother who gets lumbered with the title *conte* so he's definitely got bigger prospects."

"Life can be tough ..." came one response.

This was not going to be easy Ignatio realised and looking around the den of nicotinic alcoholic comfort frequented by men and women on the same quest, companionship and a laugh, an idea came to him. He got up on a chair as though it were the most natural thing in the world and asked if anyone there could guarantee the successful conclusion to a proposal to his *ragazza, Signor* Farangio's *figlia maggiore,* just in case she had it in mind to be a bit 'difficult.' At this he climbed up on to the table and posing on one knee tried out a little speech and some witticisms.

His audience was not backward in coming forward with suggestions, less pointed now. Girl-meets-boy romancing is sure to get to any Italian's heart. There followed the funniest two hours any of them could remember as they related their courting days and ways in which they had proposed to their girls or *vice versa* and how it could probably have been done better.

It wasn't until after closing time that Ignatio and Lella's father settled on a plan regarding the proposal. Only when Ignatio mentioned Gabrielle liking his music hall miming did he learn that her father was a lifelong Elvis fan. He did the occasional social function in full costume miming to a CD, he said.

It was very late when *Signor* Farangio next looked at the clock over the bar. Ignatio was well-incapable of driving by then, backwards or forwards and he took the lad's keys. Ignatio hadn't noticed Lella's father had hardly been drinking.

"You were very adult, coming out to see me," he said quietly. "Now I know you're a good sort I will get used to you as my *genero*. The least I can do is show more responsibility to you young ones. I'm taking you home in the van."

The musical interlude in the drawing room after supper on Christmas Day began with one of Clementino's friends tackling a dark, discordant Gesualdo madrigal, accompanying himself on the harpsichord. This was followed by a much brighter recorder and flute arrangement of a Corelli trumpet sonata. Sophie eventually livened things up with a reading of a passage from a classic work, *Una Donne* by one of her feminist heroines Sibilla Aleramo. It wasn't so much the literature, more the way in which she was dressed.

As she strutted around the stage with great fire and passion in a tiny red *Babbo Natale* costume trimmed with white fur and a tinsel scarf in full flow, Clementino for some artistic reason had the spotlight focussed on her bare legs. When Sophie caught on she began crouching to get her face and the book in the light. Soon laughter eclipsed the drama of the passage she was reading.

Most people in the room had read Aleramo's book. None were more appreciative than Ferdinand at the back of the drawing room behind the stage. His cousin Anna had her arm through his. He shouted *bravo!* a couple of times at the end of the reading and Sophie turned and thanked the couple, the count and countess, actually their host and hostess that Christmas with a magnificent bow.

Clementino, on his toes, caught the moment the little Santa costume was of no use whatsoever in covering her bottom, to tumultuous whistling and cheering from those who appreciated such frissons as a leggy lady showing silk knickers. Or, as Tel referred to it, *Top Totty showing her best china.*

What better warm-up could Elvis have wished for. The foot-stamping and slow handclap began for the new star turn that evening. The lights dimmed and the one and only, the fabulous *Signor* Elvis in a perfect white and silver lamé jump-suit shuffled across the stage belting out "you ain't nothin' but a hound dog ..." to an impossibly loud music track. He went through everything expected by a provincial audience, hip gyration, leg-wobbling and a final circular swinging of his microphone. He was good, as his eldest daughter had promised and she was so proud of him.

When he had finished he said breathlessly into the microphone over the applause, that was him done for the night. It was a rare occasion, a very special night when he was actually a support act. He would now make way for someone even more special, a younger man with the voice, looks and charisma all the girls would fall for. Well, one in particular ...

The lights dimmed again and the strangest of duets began, "Love me tender, love me sweet, never let me go ..." with a simultaneous *"Amami teneramente, amami dolce, non lasciarmi mai andare ..."*

Gabrielle put her hand to her mouth. The spotlight picked up the miniature doppelganger accompanying Elvis in Italian. He was also in a tight jumpsuit, mostly of silver. The hair was perfect, as was the smile, the sideburns, the sultry look.

There was much whistling and as Ignatio got into his stride a very large box with green ribbon around it was slid towards him. It wouldn't have surprised the audience if a girl in a plumed head dress jumped out of it clad only in tinsel. A white Conti board with marker pens followed.

"... for my darlin' I love you, and I always will ... *per il mio tesoro ti amo, e lo farò sempre."*

While still singing, Ignatio scribbled a message on the board and held it up for Gabrielle specifically. She was on her feet. *Picci* had written the magic words a girl dreams of hearing, or reading in this instance,

"Ti amo. Mi vuoi sposare?"

He then went down on one knee, gesturing to his girl, then the box. She rushed on stage squealing, ignoring the box and threw herself at him, sending them both sprawling. Ignatio carried on crooning regardless on the floor, on his back. Gabrielle grabbed the board and scribbled,

"Si, si, grazie! grazie! xx"

"... for it's there that I belong, and we'll never part ... *perché è lì che io appartengo, e ce la faremo mai parte ...*"

Ignatio gestured again to the box against which someone had placed a chair. He then wrote on the board to more laughter, *"lo spettacolo deve andare avanti!"*

"Never mind 'the show must go on' *stupido*," roared one of his friends, "just pick her up and put her in your pocket!"

"... Love me tender, love me true, all my dreams fulfilled ... *Amami teneramente, amami vero, tutti i miei sogni si sono realizzati ...*"

Gabrielle stood on the chair, opened the box and reaching inside fell into it in an unladylike manner. She emerged triumphant, clutching a tiny version also with a green ribbon around it. Ignatio gestured she open it.

"... Love me tender, love me dear, tell me you are mine. I'll be yours through all the years, till the end of time ... Love me tender, *amarmi cara, dimmi che sei mia. Sarò tua per tutti gli anni, fino alla fine dei tempi ...*"

Her eyes shining, she held up a ring for all to see, a huge oval cut emerald surrounded by diamonds. Clementino zoomed in on it. Gasps and cheering were heard over Elvis and Ignatio. Gabrielle rushed over to *Picci* again and grabbed him. Determined to the last, he just managed,

"... *tutti i miei sogni soddisfano. Per il mio tesoro ti amo, e lo farò sempre,*" with the real Elvis adding "... all my dreams fulfil. For my darlin' I love you, and I always will."

Gabrielle was so excited tears were rolling down her cheeks. When the song finished Ignatio slipped the ring on her finger and they stood there in the spotlight clinging to each other to cheers and great applause. Now she was just sobbing.

By midnight, at about the right time for Christmas Day to end, it was blissfully quiet in the house for the first time in days. People were still up playing cards. There was chatting, chatting up, some music playing softly and a game of billiards in progress.

"A fortunate young man. And woman, I am bound to say. She was so proud showing her engagement ring," Vespucci said to his cousin with whom he was having a last drink by the fire.

"An exceptional Columbian *Muzo* stone of three point two carats. There are one-and-a-half carats of diamonds around it set in eighteen carat gold on a platinum band. That's eight thousand dollars a carat retail for the emerald ..."

"... *Prego! Prego!*" Vespucci interrupted, with a gentle smile. "You, my boy, did well. You advised, I assume?"

"My favourite stones, cousin, as you know," Anna purred. "We had a long chat in the Summer, Ignatio and I. He vowed he would propose before the end of this year whatever the circumstances. He made up his mind on the day they met about a stone colour matching the little lady's eyes. So touching. I had the three best jewellers in town bring their finest wares to the *palazzo*. And I stand no nonsense with prices, as you also know."

"No, no, cousin, of course not."

"This pretty *fidanzata* will give her all. You do when you are young. You are not so old you are forgetting such things, cousin!"

It was midnight when Ignatio and Gabrielle slipped on coat, hat, woollen socks and Wellingtons and ventured outside. It had stopped snowing, the sky was clear, the moon up and the temperature 12 degrees below and falling. They wanted to see how deep the snow was and admire the stars on Christmas Night in the mountains of Lombardy.

They strolled through the door arm in arm but beyond the porch began running through the drifts, past the tractor shed and up the track to 1783, laughing all the way. Breathing hard, both dropped flat on their backs in the snow beneath the stone lintel that meant so much to them.

Moments later Ignatio's *ragazza, fidanzata* his *promesso* was up again and kneeling by him. To his surprise and one that made him gasp she hitched up her skirt and sat astride him pushing him gently back into the snow. For a moment he didn't know what she was doing, until the moonlight caught a little smile, her eyes glinting and the flash of diamonds and emerald as she held up the back of her hand for him to admire the ring. She arranged her coat around them to keep the cold out, a little tent in the snow in a perfect silent night on the hillside.

Rocking very gently she asked, "do you like my perfume?"

He nodded vigorously.

"Coco Mademoiselle, for my *Monsieur* at Christmas."

"... like hot plum pudding and ice cream ..."

With the slightest shimmying of her breasts that all but melted the snow around them she said "now I want to introduce you to my two girls. They have been waiting to meet you, asking why it has been so long. Three years, one month and two days. Soon they will officially be yours ..."

Unbuttoning her cardigan slowly she began singing softly in English, *"... Love me tender, love me true, all my dreams fulfil. For my darlin' I love you ..."*

www.ingramcontent.com/pod-product-compliance
Lightning Source LLC
Chambersburg PA
CBHW071714140626
46557CB00011B/223